HIDING PLACE

HIDING PLACE

JOHN EDGAR WIDEMAN

VINTAGE BOOKS

A DIVISION OF RANDOM HOUSE   NEW YORK

Library of Congress Cataloging-in-Publication Data
Wideman, John Edgar.
Hiding place.
Originally published: New York: Avon Books, 1981.
I. Title.
PS3573.I26H5   1988   813'.54   88-40125
ISBN 0-679-72027-8 (pbk.)

Manufactured in the United States of America
10 9 8 7 6 5 4 3 2 1

For Mort, Elise, and Takajo
Special spirits . . . special place.

Went to the Rock to hide my face
Rock cried out, No hiding place

AFRO-AMERICAN SPIRITUAL

FAMILY TREE

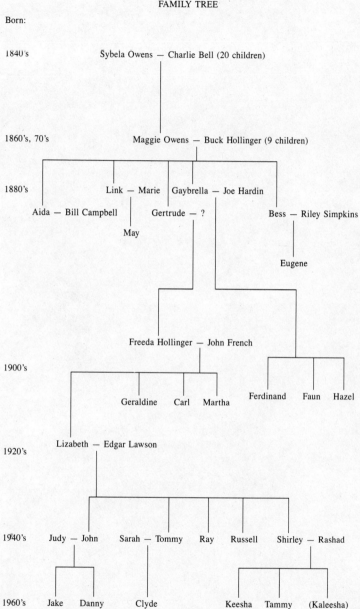

Born:

1840's   Sybela Owens — Charlie Bell (20 children)

1860's, 70's   Maggie Owens — Buck Hollinger (9 children)

1880's   Link — Marie   Gaybrella — Joe Hardin

Aida — Bill Campbell   Gertrude — ?   Bess — Riley Simpkins

May

Eugene

Freeda Hollinger — John French

1900's   Geraldine   Carl   Martha   Ferdinand   Faun   Hazel

1920's   Lizabeth — Edgar Lawson

1940's   Judy — John   Sarah — Tommy   Ray   Russell   Shirley — Rashad

1960's   Jake   Danny   Clyde   Keesha   Tammy   (Kaleesha)

I

CLEMENT

▼▼

Clement listened to them talk. Two men dead. Niggers caught, and niggers running away. He snorted some of that nasty stuff down out his head. Tasted like blood in his raw throat but he swallowed because ain't no place to spit. Full this morning. Head felt like a bucket of soggy grits. Couldn't keep his eyes dry for blinking and the snot rag balled in his back pocket had been folded and refolded so many times he didn't want to touch it anymore.

He knew that if he waited long enough somebody would want something. So he listened to the men tell each other lies. Morning lies that were slow and lazy as worms. Everybody still too evil to laugh and joke so somebody would mutter something under his breath like he was just talking to hisself but if you listened you'd know he was lying and wanted somebody to hear it. So there they were, those lazy morning lies all over the floor of the barbershop, spotting the marbled green squares of linoleum like the hair balls later on in the day.

Clement sees the floor covered with kinky, matted hair. Then he is a broom whisking it into a pile in the corner away from the door. You get it just about up and some fool come swinging in the door and jiving back over his shoulder and you got to begin all over again, the wind catch that hair and start it to flying and rolling.

He listens to Al who says the Hi Hat was jumping last night. He listens to Lloyd describe the size of the knot he put upside his old lady's head when she told him there wasn't no coffee in the house to be made and that's why she was laying up in bed like the Queen of Sheba or Miss Ann or some gawdamn body like she ain't got good sense. Clement listens and watches the lies squirm and wiggle across the floor. That spit-stained,

13

foot-scuffed, cigarette-butt-burned, hair-growing floor he knows every inch of.

Big Bob's hands in the mirror behind his back, tying the green smock. If hands had eyes they would watch themselves pull the string tight and make a bow above Big Bob's fat ass. But hands needed eyes to do something behind your back when you're not looking so Clement tried to catch them looking at themselves in the mirror. Winking maybe at theyself cause they got the bow so nice and even. In the mirror you could see the back of Bob's sign. The dusty backside of the sign and see it backwards too. BIG BOB that would light up red except the last big "B" so it was BO when it was red, BIG BO like Little Bo Peep and her sheep.

And see black wool all over the floor if you stood up close to the mirror and looked down into it, dreaming down into it, past the spots and dull, cracked edges, past the clots of curling Bo Peep black sheep wool, dreaming while the broom goes on about its business and the voices of the men are coming at you from far away like there is something like a mirror and the voices sink into it then leak out again far away so when you hear them it's not the men you hear now but the men talking yesterday or a week ago somewhere inside something like a mirror.

Hey, Clement. Get your butt up off that chair, boy. Them chairs for my customers, you know that. If you gon sleep, go on in the back.

Aw leave em lone, Bob. He ain't doing nothing but dreaming up on a little pussy.

Nothing is what that lazy nigger be doing all the time.

You too hard on the boy.

I keep a roof over his head and food in his mouth. Now if that's hard I sure would appreciate somebody being hard on me. Wouldn't be out here at dawn dealing with all you nappy-head niggers.

Ain't no way to talk to the public.

Yeah, Bob. You talk nasty we gon take our business elsewhere.

Sure nuff.

Why don't you do just that. Why don't youall go over to Mr. Tivoli's. Go on over there so he can run you out with that shotgun he keeps for parting colored folks' hair.

You know we love you, Big Bob. Ain't gon leave you for no dago.

Even though you can't cut hair a lick.

Even though you talk about folks like a dog.

Even though I ain't had a hit since I been playing my figure here.

Just cause your number is trifling as you is Burgess, ain't no reason to blame me. Big Bob always pays. You play, I pay.

Clement. Simple as you is, boy, you ought to be lucky. Gimme a number to play, Clement.

Play your mama.

What you say, boy?

You heard em. You heard em good and plain just like everybody else did.

Sure nuff told you what to play.

Don't care if you's feebleminded you little scrufty pick-aninny. I'll go upside your burr head you start playing the Dozens at me.

You asked him what to play...

And he told you.

Yes he did.

What's your mama's name, Burgess? Big Bob, look up his mama's name in the book.

Which book you talking about?

Ow, wheee.

You see that. You niggers always signifying.

You the one said *what book*. You the one playing Dozens and putting people's mamas' names in little black books people carry round in their hip pockets.

You all just getting deeper and deeper.

Go on and look it up in the Dream Book.

Just leave it alone now. It's too early in the morning for this mess.

Simpleminded or not, that boy better watch his mouth.

Clement don't mean no harm. Here boy. Tell Claudine to send me over some warm milk. These niggers is on my nerves already this morning and I gots to take my medicine.

Big Bob's hand is studded with eyes. They are hidden in the folds of his dumpling-colored palm. If he opened his hand wide Clement knew they'd be there staring up at him. *No Sale* sits in the long window of the cash register. Big Bob slams it shut with his other hand as Clement takes the quarter from his plump fingers.

It was too early in the morning to talk about people's mamas. Since Clement never had a mama he could remember it was never too early or too late or any time at all to talk about his. Clement wondered if she was alive or dead. If he ever passed her in the Homewood streets and didn't even know it was his own mama who was smiling or cut her eyes at him or flounced past him, through him, dressed to kill on somebody's arm like her son wasn't even on the pavement. He believed his mama wore perfume. But when he tried to understand its smell all he could think of was the pomade- and lather-thick air of Big Bob's. He knew she would smell good. Not good like the men thought they smelled when Big Bob splashed his hands with lotion from the tall, colored bottles and slapped his hands together and patted it on their bumpy necks. A different good. A real good. Like some women Clement passed on the street. Or some of the women who came in Bob's to play their numbers.

He knew she'd smell good and speak softly. There be nothing bout her to make the men laugh or talk nasty so he would never hear them mention his mama's name in the barbershop. Anyway his mama had no name except the secret one he carried in his heart, the name he would never say, except to himself quietly in the middle of the night when he was almost asleep in Big Bob's backroom. Never say it to anyone even if somebody held a .357 magnum to his head and said *Say it or die, nigger* he wouldn't say her secret name because then somebody else could say it and touch her and he'd have to snatch one of Big Bob's straight razors and slit the nigger's throat.

If he had a razor long enough and needle-thin enough Clement would poke it up his nose hole and puncture the swollen bag of stuff clogging his head. It hurt to think on mornings like this when his head so full it would roll down off his shoulders and he'd need both hands to pick it up and press it back where it belonged.

Wouldn't smell his mama if she be sitting on his face. Not this morning. Her perfume, whatever it was like, be wasted on him this miserable sinus-thick morning. Clement thought of blind noses and blind hands, how they couldn't see any better than Mr. Raymond sitting there behind his big green shades on the corner rattling his cup and selling those yellow pencils with the gum band round them nobody takes when they drop in a penny. Clement had heard the men say Old Mr. Raymond bring you luck you drop a big piece of money in his coffee can after you have a good night and the bones been talking for you. Say it pleases your luck when you spread it around, say your luck will come back double you treat it right so some days you might see a hundred-dollar bill in that can. But anything can be blind as Mr. Raymond. Noses and hands and feet and ears. Even your mouth could be blind when your talk is heavy and your behind light. Or when you can't talk at all. Just sit and listen at the men's voices coming from far away while you sweep and the mirrors catch on fire and everybody in Big Bob's burning up but you can't say nothing cause your mouth is blind and you be burning up too.

Miss Claudine, Big Bob want his warm milk.

Good morning, Clement.

Good morning, Miss Claudine. I forgot again, Miss Claudine.

Nice folks don't put their *Gimmes* before their *Good mornings*. Now how many times have I told you that.

I'm sorry, Miss Claudine.

Least you remember the *Miss*. Which is a lot better than plenty of these supposed-to-be-grown-ups running around here who should know better. A little etiquette don't cost a cent. A little respect for people don't cost a thin dime and it can make a person feel like a million dollars. That's what I try to tell these gimme this and gimme that negroes always busting in here in such a hurry. Don't I be telling them all day, Mr. Lavender?

She sure does.

And you'd think since it's *free*, people'd be free in passing out a little respect. But here they come. Mouthful of gimme and hardly a much obliged passing they lips.

I'ma remember that *Good morning* next time, Miss Claudine.

You a good boy, Clement. You kinda forgetful but you a good boy. You better than you should be, growing up mongst that low-life riffraff hanging round the barbershop. You got the worst element in the community right there. Somebody needs to throw a bomb in there one Saturday afternoon about four o'clock. Rid the neighborhood of ninety-nine percent of its pimps and hustlers and dope peddlers and no-goods. I'd buy

the bomb. Yessir, you find me a person got the heart to throw
it and poor as I am I'll buy the bomb. Wonder as you ain't
worse than you is, living the kind of life you do. It ain't your
fault. You's a good boy and you seems to try hard even if you
ain't got much sense to try with. Milk'll be a minute heating
up. Tell that evil Big Bob what I said, too. Wish his overweight
doughnut-butt self was right here now and I'd tell him to his
face.

Mr. Lavender. Give this child one of them pastries. With
the jelly on top like he likes. Look at you grinning from ear
to ear. Wish I had room to take you in. But I done had all the
children I'm gon have. Got grandchildren staying with me now.
Got my hands full with my own babies or else I'd take you out
of that hellhole.

Thank you, Mr. Lavender, and ain't he cute saying *thank
you* just like I taught him. That's the kind you like ain't it,
sugar. Go on and enjoy it, but take a napkin and keep your
chin clean and wipe your hands when you done.

Here now. You tell Bob Henderson I didn't put no arsenic
in it this morning. But you tell that blubberbutt, pigeon-toed
excuse for a man I'm gon fix him good one day. Got a jar full
of poison with his name on it. And tell him I'd buy the bomb.

Clement watches her fit the lid on the styrofoam cup. Her
purple finger circles three times, twice softly pressing on the
lid and once more spiraling in the air just above the sealed lips
of the cup. He won't repeat to Big Bob anything Miss Claudine
has said. He doesn't need to because Big Bob hears every
word. She still loves me don't she, boy. She's still talking trash
ain't she. That old Biddy would cut my heart out if she could.
Cut it out and put it on a platter and just sit there and die happy
looking at my heart on her platter on her table in her kitchen.
We go back a long way. Thirty years if it's a day and she ain't
never forgived or forgot Big Bob. But you don't know what
I'm talking bout do you, boy. Just words to you ain't it, boy.
Love just a word to you.

It's hot now. Be careful how you hold it. Don't spill it on
yourself.

Thank you, Miss Claudine.

Don't you forget to tell him what I said.

But Clement knows he won't tell, knows he doesn't have
to. He giggles to himself as his feet hit Homewood Avenue

again. Giggles because he is carrying Big Bob in a little white cup. He can feel him splashing around inside. Big Bob laughing because he's heard every word Miss Claudine said.

Most mornings Miss Claudine takes the quarter but sometimes she says you put that back in your pocket. I know that skinflinty Negro don't never give you no spending change. She took it this morning when she handed him the cup full of Big Bob so Clement does not detour to the Brass Rail where anybody who can reach the counter can buy a glass of sweet wine they got a quarter to pay for it. He goes straight down Homewood a block and a half and pushes through the door of Big Bob's. The bell jingles to greet him just as it had jingled when he left. Good-bye and hello, the same thing if it's the bell talking.

Big Bob takes the cup and winks at Clement. The wink is good-bye and hello, no difference, just like the bell.

Old biddy still loves me, don't she. Milk's nice and warm as toasted titty.

He unlocks the cabinet below the cash register and hauls out the J&B by its skinny green neck. Two inches of warm milk splash into the sink and then the cup is brimful again as scotch rides the milk. Big Bob blows on the mixture, brews it with his little finger. He drains the cup slowly, steadily, never lowering it from his lips. His eyes are closed and his head tilted back on his shoulders so the rolls at the back of his neck swallow the collar of his polka-dot shirt.

Hmmmmmm. A man needs some strong medicine fortify his nerves in the morning. Specially if he got to deal all day with black folks.

Clement wishes he was the empty cup. Somebody needs to open the top of his head and pour out all the nasty stuff up there. It would be so thick and greasy in the sink bowl you'd have to wash it away with a blast from the spigot.

Not so bad now that he had been up awhile and walked to Miss Claudine's and back. Cold walks opened him up faster, but it would be a long time before he'd be taking cold walks. Just the middle of May but the weather had turned and already Clement had forgotten that the streets ever had been or ever again would be so bone-cracking cold he'd just want to curl up and die. Can't remember winter when it's summer and can't remember summer when it's winter. Ain't never been no winter and never be such a thing again when he trudges with his ears sweating and the hot ground coming up through his sneakers to the top of Bruston Hill to the old woman's house.

Clement would listen to the men talk a while longer. Wait and see if anybody wanted anything else. He'd run their errands and take whatever they'd tip him, and check out the Brass Rail, but then he'd go up Bruston Hill. Walk to the very top where she lived. He hears Miss Bess listening for his feet hit her raggedy porch. Miss Bess waiting on the top of Bruston Hill. Everything in him blind except the part hearing her silent call.

BESS

▼▼▼

It was spring and she was a girl again. A beautiful long-haired
young girl again. She could watch and listen because somebody
was telling a story about her. Maybe it was Aida talking. Little
Aida whose feet never touched the floor when she sat in a
chair. Aida would tell it wrong. She'd get days mixed up, and
people's names all funny and sometimes you'd have to stop
her and ask What'd you say girl because Aida could take a
word and turn it inside out so Jesus hisself wouldn't know what
that child be talking about. Aida thought it was cute. Talked
baby talk longer than she should have, and what she used to
do because she thought it was cute got to be a habit and now
she's an old woman and you got to stop her just like you would
a child and say What's that you said, say Stop a minute, Aida,
I don't know what in the world you're talking about and Aida
just smile her ain't-I-cute smile and wiggle her feet that still
don't touch the floor and keep on telling her story like she ain't
old as I am and should know better.

Could be somebody else telling it so she does not interrupt,
does not try to pick out the voice, just watches and listens.
Because in the story she is young and beautiful and the sky is
like a pretty picture above her and green, green grass is under
the blanket on which she's sitting in her white Sunday dress.
She is not seeing any of that at the moment because her eyes
are closed and her arms are stretched behind her and her throat
and forehead are bare to the sun and the sun is a warm kiss
putting her to sleep. What she saw last before her eyes shut
were birds flying high above the trees. Birds so high they were
black specks wheeling in formation, a handful of dark seeds
scattered by an invisible hand.

Then the singing, just as she'd heard it the night before, in

21

the terrible, floating space before sleep mercifully severed her head from her body.

Farther along . . . Farther along.

That old preacher, dead these many years, singing her man's song. Black Frank Felder, his big head like a bowling ball above the white collar, his tiny eyes squeezed shut, his mouth pained, busy at the corners like he's trying to talk to hisself while he's singing the words of the hymn.

Farther along we'll know more about you.

Ain't no doubt about it. He can sing. Yes he can now. Ain't no better than none them other chicken-stealing holy rollers but that man can chirp, Bess.

Her man would sit on the back step of Homewood A.M.E. Zion Church. He'd sit all Sunday morning back there in the alley with the cats and garbage cans to catch Frank Felder singing.

Farther along.

The song in the story just like it'd been in the dream, which wasn't a dream but the edge of a stormy sea, tossing, wailing, shaking her soul like a leaf till she drowned in sleep. The singing calm and peaceful as she leaned back on her hands and the weight of her body rested in her shoulders, and the weight was no burden, but was knowledge that she was strong and young and beautiful under her clothes under a picture-perfect sky. Her fingertips tickled the nappy grass where it escaped the edge of the blanket spread out beneath her to preserve her long, white Sunday dress.

He'll understand why.

The singing is part of the story she is watching and hearing as somebody tells it, somebody not her because she doesn't believe anything anymore. Not even enough to make stories. Especially stories where she can be young, can be anything but what she is at the top of this hill where everything began and she is nothing. Nothing now in the morning, nothing in the storms before sleep but somebody waiting to die. Yes. Yes.

Once upon a time her man whispered in her ear that she was silk and honey. Whispered and touched her so she turned to just what he said she was. Half wake under the blankets she could be anything, could be silk and honey and satin in his arms, in his hands when it wasn't morning yet, but not night either. A young once upon a time woman in his brown sleep-thick eyes. He was twenty years older than she was and always would be he said when he asked her to run away with him, asked her to marry him forever. But he never said forever. He said Baby I'm twenty years older than you and always will be. It don't seem much now, but it will later. Won't get no better, that's for sure. So if you take me now, you'll be taking those twenty years and those twenty years won't never go away. And she thought, One day. She thought, One morning, one night, one day is all that matters. And she was right. And he was right. The morning was magic and she was everything, anything he needed her to be. Though his eyes were puffy, and the stubble on his cheeks and chin would redden her skin, her silk and honey where he nuzzled her in the morning. Twenty years nothing at all. Twenty years everything whenever her man was gone and she asked herself, couldn't help asking herself, if he'd ever return.

Farther . . . Farther.

She used to hear: *Father. Father Along.* Like it was a name. A name for God or Jesus or whoever they thought they were singing to. And the man they sung to had a face, a walk, a way of making her feel when she pictured him, sang about him herself. Then she saw the song written in one of the hymnals stamped A.M.E.Z. in gold on the spine. It wasn't until they moved to the new church. She was grown by then but still thought everybody sang *Father. Father Along.* All the songs she'd learned, she'd learned by hearing the others sing. But in the new church they bought when the white people started running away from Homewood there were benches and metal racks on the slanting backs of the benches and in these racks were hymnals and prayer books and fàns decorated with Bible verses and pictures from Sunday School books and the names of funeral parlors. In the stiff-backed black book with pages like tissue paper it was *Farther, Farther Along.* She had to read it twice to make sure. She thought it might be a different song, believed it had to be different from the one she'd been hearing and singing all her life, but it wasn't so she lost her Father Along, lost his smile, his infinite forgiveness, his dance, strut, glide, stomp, gentle walk, his brown eyes and the tender sweep of his garment. She lost her God.

Then it was her man. Her man's song, her man in the song, her man's voice blended with all the other singers when she heard it. She was afraid at first. Afraid of thunderbolts and crackling lightning because she thought about her man's hands,

her man's breath whenever the others sang. She took what was
holy and tucked it in bed beside her and loved it and let it love
her and she was afraid for a long time. Perhaps always was,
always will be. Perhaps she had been struck down just as part
of her believed she should be, would be. Down couldn't be
any further, any farther along than the top of this lonely hill
where it all had begun and where she was dying.

But she was young again and it was spring and she'd listen
till whoever was telling the story got tired of telling it.

Her fingers played in the coarse grass. Over her shoulder,
up the slope and to the left toward the train tracks and the foot
bridge, she could hear the chains of the swings creaking. Somebody would be flying, gulping the blue air and trying to swallow
it, keep it down before the next rush, the next mouthful when
the swing soared to the end of its tether and you thought it just
might pitch you into the middle of the steel rails.

Bess . . . Bess.

It was her man calling. But he was long dead. He couldn't
be telling the story. No one was telling the story because the
sky was falling and the music dying and her man's voice was
far away now, far and high away as the birds. Her man was
a speck. A raisin, a seed, then a tiny hole in the sky like a
stone makes just for a second when it hits the water.

Bess . . . Bess.

She is saying her own name alone in the light that is not
morning yet or night still but in between somewhere so she's
not sure either has happened or will happen again. *Bess*. Saying
her name so it's like *the end* and chases the story away.

Bess, why don't you come down off that Godforsaken
hillside and stay with us. You know we'd love to have you.

It gets so bad up there in winter. Some days nobody could
get up there to help you, don't care how hard they tried.

Winter is gone. Is someplace else. Not winter hands she is
lifting to her face. Winter hands are cold and stiff. They sleep
under a pile of rocks and the bruising rocks are packed in snow.
You are barely able to light the stove with winter fingers. If
you held them in the fire they would weep and crackle, but
you wouldn't feel a thing, can't feel a thing for half the morning
sometimes, then it's just the pain of thawing, of having them
crippled and sore again at the ends of your arms.

That is how you begin feeling sorry for yourself. When you
pity a hand, or a finger, or a foot that's so pitiful anybody

would be sorry for it whether it was theirs or somebody else's.
When part of you gets so pitiful it's just pitiful and nothing to
do with you, just a pitiful thing laying there beside a coffee
cup, too swollen and crippled up to raise the cup, then you
know somebody's in trouble and you know it's you and you
can't help but feel sorry.

Some mornings I got no feeling at all in my hands or my
feet.

Sounds like poor circulation to me. Your heart's just not
pumping blood the way it used to. Takes the blood a little
longer to get everywhere it's supposed to be.

Some mornings it ain't just hands and feet. Seems like I got
a rubber band or something too tight on my arms and legs.
Some mornings them bands creep up farther and farther and
it's like I'm turning to stone. Like they might just keep sliding
up and won't be nothing left with feeling.

You need to come down off that hill. I bet half those aches
and pains would go away if you come down off that hill.

As if those lights, those streets, that noise . . .

She can feel her hands under the quilt. Feel enough to know
they are twisted and sore but not frozen winter hands. She
wiggles her toes and counts all ten little piggies down there.
Only one man ever touched her toes. Only one man counted
them and took each one between his teeth and nibbled it, wig-
gled it and tried to chant the nursery rhyme with his mouth full
of foot. But she says *Bess* again. And Bess is what she is now.
Alone now at the top of Bruston Hill. Her veins draw the chill,
carry the deadness from her limbs to the center of her body,
to the place she never knew she had until her son borning took
it away with him. There the flow converges, stops there in a
lake or a pool that is blacker and deeper than night. There she
feels nothing but the guttering in and the depth of the hole into
which the icy waters spill.

At least get a phone up here, Mother Bess. Then if you get
in trouble you can call one of us. And we could call you up
every once in a while to check in.

Telephone in my bosom is what she thinks but does not say
to her great-niece or granddaughter-in-law or whatever she
is . . . This flimsy thing in pants and a blouse with too many
colors like a African or some other old country fool be wearing.
Drive up Bruston Hill like a man and got a man's pants hugging
her narrow hips, showing her butt and skimpy drawers. Tele-

phone in my bosom she started to say. And I can ring him up
any time. But this little chocolate thing wouldn't know what
I be talking about. And if she did know, think I still got religion.
But it's just a song. Just something come to mind. And I ain't
got no business saying it out loud. Ain't no Christian or nothing.
Like she ain't got no business saying *trouble*. Nobody drive
up Bruston Hill and wear pants like a man knows what trouble
is. Trouble on the seat beside her but she don't know trouble.

Get on out here, girl. Cousin whoever you is. Your skimpy
underwear's showing. Now go on and tell all them folks down
there about trouble. About that crazy old bad-mouthed lady
don't appreciate nothing.

She can smell the stink of spring. How everything the ice
and snow kept covered all winter is outside again rotting, getting soft underfoot. The mud will stick to her shoes. Rising
from the streets below the sour smell of garbage the trash men
spill, the mess people toss out their windows and back doors.
People sneak up on Bruston Hill with truckloads of God knows
what and dump it wherever they please. Soon the rains will
come and begin to wash the mess back down where it came
from, where it belongs. The gutters will overflow and milk
cartons and cans and bones and cigarette butts and every kind
of filth get stuck in the broken cobblestones stinking till more
rain carries it away. And brings more.

Soon she won't have to light the stove in the morning. The
wooden walls will get dark with sweat. Get loose and runny
like everything does in spring. Then the dog days will turn her
house into an oven. She'll sit from early morning till night on
what's left of the porch, in what's left of her rocker, in what's
left of her body. The house is a piece of clothing she has been
wearing all these years. Like her wool sweater with holes in
the elbows and patches and worn places thin and see-through
as cellophane. The house like a sweater somebody painted on
her body so she can't take it off. Not to patch or wash or give
it a vacation. The house is painted on, stitched to her skin,
wool threads and flesh threads all woven together now and she
could no more take off the raggedy sweater than she could
grab the black handle of a steam iron and press out the million
wrinkles in her face.

The seeds Clement brought her still lie where he dropped
them on the table. Packets with bright pictures of perfect vegetables she's never seen anywhere but on packages of seeds.

She'd be afraid to eat something looks like them painted tomatoes. Look more like the heart torn out some live animal,
something that bleeds and breathes and would still be thumping
in your hand when you tried to eat it. She couldn't make up
her mind about the garden. Not so much a question of planting
it or not planting it this year, but never remembering the seeds
until she sees them and then forgetting them till they flash up
at her again. Even with the pile of packets right there on the
table she sits at every day she might not see them for a week.
Sometimes she hears them. Rattling like they did when Clement
dumped them from the grocery sack.

Here they is, Miss Bess. She could hear them scratching
to get out.

Late now for putting seeds in the ground. There was a time
they turned the ground from the back porch all the way to the
trees at the edge of the hill. Long straight furrows combed in
the earth and they'd grow enough to can and get through the
winter. Beans and peas and tomatoes and cucumbers and lettuce
and turnips and mustard greens. Sticks marching in regular
rows and strings stretched for the vines to climb. Corn and
grapes and parsley. Once her brothers had shown her where
sausage grew and the hole where she should lay the hambone
and cover it with ash to grow a new ham. You see anything
yet? Ought to be sprouting up pretty soon now. You sure you
spread them ashes careful? You sure you been watering it every
day? Maybe you put your ear to the ground you hear it oinking.
A fence then to keep out stray dogs and cats. Raccoons still
around too. Her daddy kept a shotgun in the cupboard but never
got a shot at one. They thought they might catch one in their
pigeon trap and baited it with bacon instead of bread but nobody
was allowed to sit up all night and hold the string which was
attached to the stick which held the box up in the air. None
of the children could stay up all night at the window to pull
the string when the raccoon went after the bacon under the
box, so we never catched one either.

Spring smelled different then. So many things growing that
nobody had planted. Sunflowers and goldenrods and pale little
flowers she didn't know the names of. Trees and weeds and
bushes. Like being in the country up on Bruston Hill. If somebody had asked her she might have claimed she lived on a
farm.

In the daytime now a brownish cloud hovered over the

purple-grey city below. The sprawl of city had its own distant
sky, more roof than sky clamped over the wobbly hills. At
night the city slept with its lights on. When you stood beneath
the trees at the edge of the hill which marked the end of their
garden, one star-sprinkled sky arched above you and another
sky crowded by blinking stars lay at your feet. If you crushed
something green and growing and rubbed the juice over your
hands spring used to smell like that. A little sweet, a little sour,
itchy almost and clinging like garlic because it's still there
hours later if you pass your finger under your nose.

She had loved to dig in the ground then. On her hands and
knees or flopped down flat on her belly if nobody was watching.
Loved to dig in those days and loved to bury things. Hambones
or any other foolishness. For a long time she believed anything
she planted would grow. She was patient, in no hurry at all.
She'd forget most of the things she had dug a home for and
covered over, but forgetting them didn't mean she believed
they'd never appear again. It just meant she'd be surprised.
Surprised at how busy she'd been. How much she had cradled
in the black earth.

Look at that child. Get up out that dirt, girl.

She gon dig a hole to China with her busy self.

Don't you get a inch closer to them beans, girl. Your
father'll fix you good you dig up any of his beans.

She was the youngest so everybody had the job of watching
over her. She was the youngest and always would be even
though most the others dead now, buried now like they'd
watched her bury tin cans and rusty spoons and leaves and just
about anything she could get her hands on if somebody didn't
keep an eye on her. And somebody always did. Even Mother
Owens who everybody said couldn't see a thing no more, even
her rocking on the porch, draped in the black cape she wore
summer spring winter and fall, even Mother Sybela Owens's
blind eyes following her as she tunnelled to China or wherever
you get by digging all the time.

Tricked me into burying a hambone. Tricked me into trying
to grow pigs' feet and roast pork and hog maws and hog jaws
and chitterlings and snout and ears and tail and side meat and
crackling gravy.

How long has it been, how many years ago was it her
Grandmother Sybela Owens rocking on the porch and her down
in the dirt digging like a groundhog. Now it was Mother Owens

in the ground, and spring stinking, and I'll be in that rocker all day wearing this old house like Mother Owens wore that black cape. Up and back, up and back a million times till it's cool enough to go on inside. Maybe seeing what Mother Owens saw behind her blind eyes because when you rock long enough you start to look inside stead of outside and you listen to the chair and listen to things scratching and rattling like them seeds to get out. But you forget. You don't pay them no mind though they sitting right there in front your face. Gets too late then. Gets past the season for planting and then you're seeing Bess and Bess is all you see behind your eyes and all you want to see cause Bess is a stone, a dead something setting here with the rest of this mess tore out the earth and waiting for the rain to wash it away.

They talked like she was dead already. Or like she was a child, or like she just wasn't there in the room with ears and breath like the rest of them.

Mother Bess we can't let you do that.

There's nothing left up on that hill but a shack. She knows that. She knows the old place has just rotted away. She's just being unreasonable and ornery. Trying to make people feel sorry for her. I'm willing to take her in or help out any of the rest of you who do. It's our responsibility and no sense in everybody getting upset. Let's just decide what to do without a lot of fussing and tears.

She doesn't really mean she wants to stay up there. I think she wants to visit. It was her home, after all. Some of us were born there too.

Have you been up there lately?

I drive past sometimes.

Have you looked? Have you stopped and really taken a good look?

More like a doghouse than someplace for a human being to live.

That's what I mean. Everything is caved in or torn down or falling apart. Just the shell of the main part of the house is left. Niggers carted away the pipes and the fixtures and shingles and boards and anything else worth a dime.

Nobody's lived there for ten years.

Ought to take better care of the place. That property might be worth something someday.

I don't think it's even in the family anymore. There were

taxes owed when Granddaddy died and I don't think anybody ever paid them. Letters used to come to the house ever so often. I was barely making my own car note and mortgage so I didn't pay them no mind. Been years since I even seen one of those bills. City probably owns it now.

That's a shame. To just let it go like that. After all these years in the family.

Yes indeed. This family started up there. Really beautiful once up there. Member going up there when I was little. Saw Grandmother Sybela Owens in that black cape rocking on the porch. Looked just like she does in the photograph Geraldine has. Mother Owens the one run off with the white man and he stole her from his own daddy and they run off from slavery up here to Pittsburgh in the old days.

We all know the story. And now's not the time to tell it. But it's a crying shame to let go someplace been in the family so long.

Ought to thought about that twenty years ago.

Who had the money twenty years ago to do anything?

Who got it now?

Well, it doesn't matter now. It's either ours or not ours and that's water over the dam, but whether it's still in the family or not it's definitely not an old folks' home. So she's not going up there and she might as well stop thinking about that possibility. We have to decide who has room and who wants to keep her. Then she can take her pick.

Don't talk so hard, son. You're not as hard a man as you're trying to seem. Don't you see Mother Bess sitting there? We're not talking about a piece of furniture.

I'm sorry, Mama. I just don't want this to turn into one of those fussing and crying and somebody stomping around and slamming doors things.

That's the way this family does business.

And that's what's wrong. We don't take care of business. We fuss and argue and somebody wins out because they got more mouth or tears. Here we sit don't even know if the property up on Bruston Hill belongs to one of us or to the city of Pittsburgh. Now that's not what I call taking care of business.

Belongs to all of us. And always will.

Sure. Sure it does. Till the city decides one day to make it a parking lot then you'll find out real fast who it belongs to.

Not enough people up there to make no parking lot.

Oh Aunt Aida. That's not the point. The point is . . .

Point is I'm tired of youall talking all this mess. Somebody call me a cab. If none you want to take me up there I still got a little change and I can pay my own way. Walk if I have to.

Mother Bess.

Here we go.

Don't be Mother Bessing me. I ain't got to ask none of youall for nothing. I been grown a long time before most of youall was even thought about. Which one of you is gon *tell* me what I can do and what I can't do? Been out here in the world long enough to make up my own mind. You can either help me or let me alone. Don't make no nevermind to me but I'm gon up there. That's what crazy old Mother Bess gon do and you can help or get out the way.

Didn't go that day but the next morning old long-head Horton was up on the top of Bruston Hill starting to fix up that doghouse. And got some of them wild boys, them nephews, to chop the weeds. Run lectricity up there and Lawyer Lawson who ain't better than nobody just because he been to college who ain't a lawyer or God Almighty to nobody but hisself he start to calling round and finding out how much was owed and if that patch of ground still in the family. They all decided to help rather than stand in the way. Gave em all something to do awhile. Something to talk about. Teached them they better talk *to* people rather than *at* people.

Sometimes I sit here and count them. I got them on chairs like in Benson's Funeral Parlor, them folding chairs the church used to borrow on Sunday before they moved up to Homewood Avenue where the white folks used to be. I sit them down and get them quiet like they never is except at church or funerals. Get them with they mouths shut while they thinking or listening and ain't got nothing to say for a blessed minute. Then I can look at their faces. Count them while they're sitting still. Like I got an envelope of pictures and I can kind of just sort through them slow like, taking my good time cause I got all day in the rocker. Like that envelope of pictures Geraldine down on Finance Street has. Only I don't believe in no photographs. Too much like being dead when you got somebody stamped on a little piece of paper and they can't move, can't talk back, can't change, you got them trapped there and that's where they always be. Don't believe in photographs. Wouldn't have them in the house. Not even one of my man. Because that wouldn't be him. Not him nailed to no wall or pressed up in some book. His picture around here just remind me he's gone. Remind me he's dead because it wouldn't be him somebody had trapped on no scrap of paper.

But I like to count them. Count all the faces and look at them a long time so I can remember where they came from, whose eyes they got and whose nose and whose chin and whose color. I can get way back. Count those faces and count all the faces who been carrying the French eyes since somebody invented those French eyes by marrying a Hollinger. I like to take my time and do that. Go way back and come up slowly through those faces I catch sitting still and run my eyes over. Sometimes I even touch them. Touch them while I got them all arranged sitting quiet in they chairs.

The sweet babies. And some almost as old as me. Takes all kinds to make my people. You pass by a couple years ago you think that old lady's crazy as a loon rocking up on that porch and grinning like a Chessy cat at herself and rocking and smacking her thigh and talking and ain't a soul up there but her. But that's my people up there and I'm coming and going and sometimes it's enough to make me laugh out loud.

Used to do a lot of that. But I been up here too long now. Too many new faces and I can't see nothing in them. No names, no places. Just faces and I think on them and all I see is Bess, myself behind my eyes and I mize well be blind as Mother Owens cause I been up here on this hill too long. They all thought I'd get tired of it or get sick or die and they could bring me down again before too long. But some's dead who said I couldn't go up on Bruston Hill and I'm still here and they don't even try anymore to talk me down. Except they say *Come down off that Hill* because that's all they got to say to me. Say those words but don't mean em. Jump ten feet in the air if I said *OK I'm coming down*. They always say *Come on down* because there ain't nothing else to say and I cut my eyes at them or say something ignorant and nasty back cause that's all I got to say. Ain't no *come down* or *stay put* to it no more. I wear this house like Sybela Owens always wore her black cape like they always gon be saying *come down* and I'm always gon be Bess and nothing else and Bess is what's up here in this chair rocking and that's all there is to it.

CLEMENT

▼▼▼

Clement heard her saying, No. He stopped in his tracks and listened at the door till he heard *No* again. Nothing strange about being miles away in Big Bob's and hearing her call him but to hear her voice on the other side of the door saying *No* or saying any damn thing, that made him freeze up in his tracks. Sound like she talking to somebody. It wasn't a crazy sound or mumbling like she sometimes does but she's saying *No* to somebody. And that didn't make sense because he'd been coming to her house for years it seemed and never in all that time had he known her to open her door to a visitor. *They just up here to neb around. They just want to prise into my business. They can come in when I'm dead. When I ain't got strength to answer the door, they can come in and bury me.* So he hesitated and waited for her to speak again or for whatever it was in there with her to answer.

That boy be coming here soon.

Who?

That boy Clement who runs to the store for me.

Don't let him in.

He got to come in.

Well, I'll go out back till he leaves.

You go out the back and stay out the back. You keep going wherever you got to go. Don't want you round here. Ain't no place for you here.

I ain't got no other place to go. Don't you understand? I tried to tell you they're after me. They probably watching every place down there by now. I got to lay low. Need some time. Need a place to hide for a little while.

No. This not gon be it. Don't want you here. Can't have you here. You done made the mess you in. Now you go on about your business and straighten it out. Go back where you came from and leave me be.

Mother Bess, I can't be walking up and down these streets in broad daylight. Don't you know what I'm talking about? Ain't you heard?

No, I ain't heard. And don't want to hear. But soon as it's dark your feets better hit the pavement. I want you out of here, boy. Do you hear me?

Till dark.

If that don't suit you, go now. Either way I want you out of here.

I'm a dead man if they catch me.

You can leave out that back door now or you can wait till it's dark. Whatever you did got the police on your tail ain't none my business. You the one they after and you the one got to answer for it. Dead is dead. You was born to die. Ain't nothing I done put the police on you. So don't be acting like I'm the one supposed to save you. It's no and that's all there is to it.

They said you was evil and crazy. That's what they always said.

No.

Aw, Mother Bess . . .

Listen at you. A grown man starting to snivel.

Clement is on his tiptoes backing away from the door. He feels like he's been standing on the crooked porch for hours, poised at the door, bobbing like a bird in slow motion up and back, his ear closer to the door then withdrawn, needing to hear and not to hear. Now he remembers for the first time how each board of the crooked porch has a mouth. How the boards squabble and squeak when he hops up to Miss Bess's door. They are as loud as Big Bob's door that rings hello and rings good-bye when you open it. For the first time he is aware of what he knew all the time because now he must ease off the porch without making a sound because it is quiet inside now, the talking has stopped and if Miss Bess wants to, she can look through the wooden walls and see him sneaking around.

Then he realizes it would be better to take one loud step forward, one loud bounce onto one of the loudest boards and call out *Miss Bess* like he always does. Then they'll know he's on the porch, at the door, instead of hearing him try to tiptoe with bells on his ankles back down the steps.

Miss Bess.

Clement can hear the man inside being suddenly more quiet than he's been since the talking stopped. He can feel the man shouting at him, *I'm not here, goddamnit*. It's OK, Clement thinks. You ain't there and I ain't gon bother you. Just gon stand here a minute and then I'm not here either.

Clement.

Yes, Mam. He can feel the man shouting. The stillness on the other side is so big you could lose all of Homewood in it. For all the sweet wine in the Brass Rail Clement wouldn't touch that doorknob, wouldn't push across the threshold and enter the shouting stillness where the old woman's eyes and the man's eyes are screaming at each other. Then she is shooing the man out the back door. Before Clement hears the familiar shuffle of her slippers there is one heavier, creaking lurch, the movement of someone who needs to pretend he is a ghost but whose first silent step nearly crashes through the floor and brings the whole raggedy house down on his shoulders.

When she opens the door Clement can't speak. He feels his face light up red as the sign in Big Bob's window. The letters flashing across his forehead tell Miss Bess everything. How he was sneaking around on the porch and listened to them talking and heard the man slip out the back. He couldn't speak and watched her read the confession burning in his cheeks and forehead.

You ready to go to the store?

Yes, Mam.

Well I ain't ready for you yet. Got to look round here and see what I need. You come by tomorrow afternoon.

Yes, Mam.

You hungry?

No, Mam.

You sick?

No, Mam.

Then what you standing there for?

Got a rock in my shoe.

Then you better sit down and take it out when you git to the bottom of the hill.

She slams the door not exactly in his face but halfway through the *mam* which he isn't saying exactly to her face but halfway over his shoulder as he turns on his heel after the *yes* and starts down Bruston Hill at exactly twice the speed her words suggested.

TOMMY

Down there they wanted to kill him. In the city streets he was
dead already. Dead as Chubby in the parking lot. Dead as
Ruchell running and hiding like there was someplace, anyplace
safe. He remembers these same tall trees from a dream or once
upon a time when he was a kid and it was night and he had
wondered how far it was to the glowing heart of the city. In
the blackness the distant lights had been white and cold. But
his hand had been warm, wrapped in somebody else's and both
of them stood staring out over the edge of the world. Somebody
had his hand and would protect him from the howling, winged
creatures who swooped through the black skies. And he had
believed he could rise on the wind and fly away, far away
where the city sparkled. Only a matter of time. Only a matter
of letting go the hand holding him under the tall trees at the
back of his cousins' house on Bruston Hill.

He could see it all now from where he stood. The stretch
of the city, how the hills flattened gradually towards the river
and climbed again to the horizon. The North Side. The South
Side. And he must be East. Because it was East End and East
Liberty and East Hills if you rode the Parkway from downtown
towards Homewood. But the city was not a map. It spread
every way at once. The city was a circle and East Liberty
niggers and Homewood niggers and West Hell niggers all the
same, all dead and dying down there on the same jive-ass
merry-go-round. All of them lost as him.

The morning haze had not lifted, would never lift. An iron-
colored cloud covered everything. Domes, steeples, spires, the
windowed towers, none of them broke through. A dirty, wet
cloud smelling like wino pee. He shivered. The chill night mist
blanketing the city had seeped inside his skin. He needed to

tell someone how tired he was, how cold, how scared. If he could say it to somebody maybe it would end. Ruchell man, it was a bitch, man. Hiding up in the Bellmawr. Creeping through all the alleys in Homewood. I'ma go back one day and strangle every one of them fucking dogs barked at me. He could see Ruchell's crooked smile. Nigger, when you gon get some teeth in your mouth. He'd tell everything to Ruchell and there'd be a wall between them and all the motherfuckers trying to kill them.

His hands were shaking, trying to get away. Told them he didn't want to be on this goddamn hill neither. Didn't want the money swirling like dead leaves around Chubby's body. If he could stop shivering, if he could tell somebody, it would all go away. Even Indovina's face. That nasty, slobbery face a speck one second and giant the next, that nightmare face he had dreamed for years and never knew its name till right here, right now on this empty hill.

He could make no sense of the city. Even in the stillness of morning, in this quiet at the top of Bruston Hill. No streets down there, nowhere to put his feet, no air to breathe. They wanted him dead down there. A slab in the morgue with his name on it. Next to Chubby, next to all the rest in neat rows in that icy room under sheets with tags on their toes. He knew about that room. Knew it was waiting. Just two blocks down from the jail. Old timers said there were secret tunnels. You could travel under the sidewalks, get there from the jail without ever leaving the underground passages.

The city was far away. Then closer than his skin. Like the face in his nightmares it shrank to a tiny spot then ballooned big enough to swallow him. The city was a stack of dishes in a sinkful of greasy water. He could stir it with his hand. Then he could hear a radio click on. Night music splitting the day wide open. He is an ear or a piece of dust or the blot of light trapped in the cup of coffee his mother carves with her spoon in the empty house. She is too hurt, too weary, too scared to cry for him anymore. A thousand of him would fit on the handle of the spoon she scrapes along the bottom of her first cup of coffee of the day. Coffee's my company she told him once. If she didn't know crazy people talked to coffee, she'd talk to hers. Her first word in that empty, falling apart kitchen be thunder and storm. Blow him away.

From where he stood at the top of Bruston Hill the only sign

of life was purplish smoke drifting from the mills along the
river, the river he couldn't see below the wedge of skyscrapers
crammed in the Golden Triangle. Once the city lights had been
mysterious, a puzzle which excited him, a design which would
stay unfinished until he made something from the scattered
pinpoints of fire. But he had been there and back; the city dust
coated his skin. It was morning again and he'd been running
and hiding all night. People were waking up. Toilets flushing,
window blinds rattling down there. Somebody barely got they
eyes open and turning on WAMO, half dead but got the Doo
Wah Diddy blasting already and lighting a match. Sonny down
there. And Sarah. They'd both know by now. They'd both
have heard the news. Somebody holier than Jesus with that I-
told-you-so look about to bust open his gums would have got
to them: Nigger ain't never been worth nothing and now he's
a killer. Now they gon kill him too.

This the top of Bruston Hill. This the place in the stories
all my people come from. He wondered how the tall trees held
on to the edge of the hill. The drop was steep, nearly perpen-
dicular. If you jumped you would tumble forever, leave a trail
of meat from the trees to the invisible river. His knees and
elbows skinned raw already. A dream had scared him awake
in the middle of the night and he had ripped open the scab
where his knee had oozed into his pantsleg. Did he scream or
was the scream in the dream too? He didn't know. Just knew
he had to get out of there. Buildings on Homewood Avenue
a poor place to hide anyway. Cops search them when they're
in the mood to beat on the winos and junkies. Scream could
have brought cops running. So when he bolted from sleep,
from the few minutes rest he had copped on the bare floor of
the old Bellmawr Show, he gritted his teeth, swallowed another
yell and crawled back down in the alley. Then alley by alley
all the way up Bruston Hill till he found the trees and ruins
and shanty.

But if he couldn't change her mind ain't found nothing.
Everybody said she was evil and crazy. He leaned back against
one of the trees. He had been here before, maybe even touched
this same tree before but nothing was familiar. Running and
hiding all night for what? To get here? To wind up nowhere?
If he had reasons for picking this jive place he surely didn't
know what they might be. Didn't know why or when his feet
decided to climb Bruston Hill. Couldn't think of any reason

now. Made it to the top but nothing said it's better now, you're OK now.

Nothing to it. Just the wooden shack she lived in and the blackened shell of the rest of the house where it had burned or collapsed or been smashed down by a giant fist. Aunt Aida said the main part of the house had burned right after the war. But she was always getting things mixed up. Talked to him one day for five minutes before he realized she thought she was talking to his sister, Shirley. He wasn't even sure which war she meant. Aunt Aida had lived through just about all the ones America ever fought. It was in World War II they said that Mother Bess had lost her son. They said she started getting funny way back then. Only had one child and that one late, like Abraham and Sarah in the Bible they said. She was near forty some when the son was born and her husband way over fifty. Nobody believed it Aunt Aida said and to top it all it was a big, healthy boy. But he died on Guam. Two days after V-J Day is the way he's heard them tell it. The Pacific war over and this Eugene, who was the only child Mother Bess had, was shot by a sniper. Said he was looking for souvenirs. Something special to bring home to his mama and this crazy Jap didn't know the war was over shot him dead on a beach six thousand miles from home.

Unless you knew there had been a big house here, you wouldn't have guessed it. Looked like somebody just patched together a shack from all the piles of junk lying around. No straight lines or even edges. Like you'd slap together a dog-house. Wall leaned one way. Little overhang of porch another. Looked like somebody had hammered together a door two sizes too small for the frame. Getting out the back when that boy came to the door he had almost stumbled over the rags she used to stuff the gap at the bottom. One back window cracked but intact, the other boarded with a tin Coca-Cola sign. Her house looked like the huts he had seen in pictures of the West Indies or South America where black people were still wild and don't live no better than animals. Shame they let her live like this. But they said she was crazy and nobody could talk her down off Bruston Hill so let her be if that's the way she wants to live, if that's how she wants to die up there by herself.

The only other thing standing in the ruins of the old place was the three-walled shed where he'd been trying to sleep. At least that was all he could see from where he stood. If he didn't know better he'd have said nobody lived here. No light coming out the house. Nothing but the smokey city below and the wild hillside plunging to meet it. Nobody else had tried to build this high on Bruston. The few houses farther down on the other side of the cobblestone street had been deserted for years. On this sloping crown of hill where the cobbles died to hard packed earth and the dirt road itself disappeared a hundred yards down the far wooded flank, nobody but his people had raised a home.

Near the shack the weeds had been chopped and the withered stubble of a garden enclosed by sticks. He didn't know how old she was but knew she was long past the age when people can dig in the ground and crawl around trying to grow things. The weeds were already thick and green. They leaned over the clear space before the sticks, shading the tangled edges of the garden. He could see where somebody had dug rows and pushed in sticks, but the garden plot looked untended, deserted like everything else.

He would go back in the shed if she wouldn't let him stay anywhere else. He was so tired he could sleep anyplace. Even standing up against these trees. If ever there had been a time in his life when he had slept long enough and untroubled enough to want to open his eyes in the morning, he had forgotten when. Sleep was a black pit and he stood with his toes on the edge and somebody kept shoving him, shoving between his shoulders so he toppled down and fell and fell and fell deeper into the darkness till his own screaming jerked him awake. Sleep had been a trap, death by falling. Yet he yearned for it. He needed to shut his eyes and forget. Then maybe it would all go away. Nobody stretched out dead on Indovina's lot. Nobody chasing him down. But all the old woman could say was *No*.

In the alleys the dogs go crazy. They come snarling at you and the big ones rear up beating their paws on the fence and barking loud enough to wake the dead. He had wanted to stop and punch one in the face, blast it and send it sniveling back under the steps where it was supposed to be asleep. Or grab one by its chain and whirl it around and around till it choked on its own spit. He had always wanted a dog. Loved dogs as a kid. But there had never been room, he never had the chance to raise one, to feed it and clean it and teach it not to shit all over the house so now dogs were just a pain in the ass. Their crap littering the streets and parks. Running at you and trying to raise the neighborhood when you're sneaking past at night.

Dogs to run you off the streets, dogs to sniff out your stash, dogs eating better than niggers, dogs to bite your dick off you get too close to them old white ladies taking their Dobermans to shit in the park.

The skinned places on his elbows and knees hurt if he moved. Couldn't see a soul in any direction and he just wanted to slip down to the ground right there with his back against a tree trunk but he'd catch hell if he bent his knees. In his shirt pocket were matches and the stub of a reefer Ruchell stuck in his hand after they ditched the van. That's all, man. We still ain't got shit, man. You take care, brother. Later, man. A toke had eased him into that little bit of sleep in the Bellmawr. Didn't care now who was hounding his ass. Too tired to care. He was going to light up. He fished out the roach. A match flared in his cupped hands and he bent to it, enjoying the sulphur stink, the fire flickering an instant against his cheek. Pulled hard on the stub till hot ash singed his lips.

My Lord, what a morning. He could hear the lead tenor of the Swan Silvertones begin the song. A husky voice but crystal clear when it hit the notes. A voice going places sweet tenor ain't supposed to be able to go. Reaching high, reaching low so *My Lord* was a king and a friend and your own jive self walking cross that Valley of the Shadow. Song bitter and sweet as the smoke, not rushing through him but marching stately as a Gospel Chorus anthem. A kind of eyes front, chest out, shake your tail-feathers, spit-and-polish clean, march-strut like they teach you drilling with the Elks Saturday in Westinghouse Park. Yes, Lawd. Ain't they fine this morning. Don't they sound good. And nobody in the Homewood A.M.E. Zion Gospel Chorus is the Reverend Claude Jeter, lead singer of the Swan Silvertones, but when some old sister shouts it out, shouts *My Lord, what a morning* from the Amen Corner don't you know the voices rise up and if Reverend Jeter ain't here he should be cause we got his song and gone. Yes, Lawd.

They want him dead. They want to kill him but he made it through the night. A thousand years of night. Haze was lifting, the sun rising behind him. Standing under the trees behind the shack of Mother Bess, a crazy, half-dead, mean old lady and he ain't got a dime in his pocket and the city a percolating vat of lye below him and every cop in Pittsburgh on his tail and he's twenty-five years old and nothing, no good just like they been telling him all the days of his life, but he is smiling, smiling maybe for the first time in his life at his own silly smile, at the top of Bruston Hill, at the silly morning being a morning here, being morning here like it's always morning someplace in the world for no good reason. Just morning, yes. Just morning. And I'm here. One more time. Yes.

BESS

▼▼

She sees his long feet poking from the corner of the shed. Long feet and fat nobby-toed shoes with heels high as a woman's. She can see that far and see that good and would thank Jesus for good eyes if she was still a Christian, but thanks nobody and praises no one's name, just stares with her good eyes at the feet protruding from the dark guts of the shed. In Highland Park Zoo she'd seen a snake once with its scaly head swoll up and the legs of a frog dangling out its jaws. Those legs were still kicking. Legs like a tiny, naked man's still kicking while that snake working at swallowing the rest. Long feet in the stub-toed shoes look like those things Minnie Mouse be wearing in the funny papers. Old-timey bubbly balloon shoes with them stick legs coming out. She can see his black socks and they make his ankles skinny black twigs. Birds all the sudden cheeping and leaping out the trees like something after them when she splashes the contents of the slop jar into the weeds. Ought to dumped it on his head. Ought to let him know just how I feel about somebody coming up here to worry me and get in my way.

The birds are settling into another tree. Like newspapers rustling. She can hear good too. Hear and see what she wants to even if there's precious little nowadays she wants to hear and see. Mize well be stone deaf and blind as a bat, mize well put her head in a bag as pay attention to what she's seen a million times before. Ought to emptied the slop jar on that fool's head. Who he think he is anyway stretched out in my woodshed like he own it?

Her long-dead sister's great-grandson's long feet in those silly shoes she can see weren't made for walking, which she can see from where she stands swinging the slop jar back and forth to air it out good, ain't made for walking and split where the sole should join the toe. If he's her sister's great-grandson he would be a... to her. He would be something she wouldn't want to claim walking around in raggedy funny-paper shoes. She knew his name and knew just exactly who he was but wasn't about to say his name to herself or to him when she kicked him on the bottom of those silly shoes and told him *Get on up from there. Go on away from here.* Wouldn't tell him nothing about what she knew. Just send him on his way. Back down to his mama's house on Finance Street if that's where the Lawsons still stayed. His brother the one thinks he knows everything. His brother the one talk like he's part God and part lawyer. Let him go on back down the hill and sleep in his brother's backyard.

She wouldn't have no milk for her coffee because of him. Needed Clement to buy milk today and needed some rolled oats and low on bread. No milk in her coffee all day and none in the first cup tomorrow morning either just because he decided to drop in on her like some long foot gorilla jump out one of these trees. If she could fly she'd do like the birds. Be gone soon's she saw him. Sit in the top of a tree till he stops hopping around and goes on about his business. But she ain't gone nowhere. She's at the top of Bruston Hill till it rots away or she rots away and you know I'm leaving here before it does. This hill been here long before Sybela Owens brought that white man from slavery. Been here longer than the city been here and longer than these trees.

She wonders what she'll be wearing on her feet when they find her and bring her down. In her trunk a pair of high topped, buttondown, hourglass-heeled ankle boots. They pushed her up four inches so she came to a different place on her man's shoulder when they were promenading arm-in-arm in Westinghouse Park and she leaned against him even though her mother would have died if she saw her daughter in public hanging like a hussy on a man's arm even if he is your husband. Those shoes, their leather yellow and soft as butter, hiked her up a good four inches and it was good to walk beside her man and have the world that little bit of distance farther away. Those yellow ankle boots were a killer. Yes they were now. Knew they looked good because she had the kind of feet to wear them. Slim, high-arched feet and trim ankles. Only one man had touched her toes. Her man nibbled them and said what she already knew but what sounded best coming from his lips. You a fine woman. A silk and honey woman. Starting here, starting right here with these little fine toes and these fine ankle bones. Yes, a killer. And she was never one to be more humble than she should. No indeed. Not with the handsomest man in Homewood right next to your ear reminding you you the finest thing walk these streets in them fancy lemon butter buttondown boots.

The boots would be in the trunk with her other things. By now the rats had probably gnawed their own doorway into the trunk and chewed up everything taste good to them. Even if rats and mice had left the trunk alone those shoes would be stiff as boards. No color left and creased and wrinkled as her face even if the rats hadn't got at them. New they was the kind of thing she'd like to be wearing on her feet when they came to take her away. Laid up in the bed fine as a fairy tale princess and the first thing they see be those tall-heeled, yellow as bananas boots. She wanted them to be surprised. That she was dead and starting to stink worse than spring wouldn't surprise nobody. But to see her in one of her fancy dresses she had cached in the trunk, fancy gown and fancy ankle boots and hair done up all nice like she's waiting for her man to take her to the Elks Ball, well, that would stop them, that would make them think a little bit before they called up the undertaker and loaded her in like a sack of potatoes. How else they think she gon meet him. He been waiting a long time and deserved the best. The first time her man sees her after all these years she wants him smiling, she wants him saying *Um umm, ain't you something, girl.*

The birds screech again and scatter again, wheeling above the tall trees clinging to the edge of Bruston Hill. She hears children squawking and squealing, the voices of her brothers and sisters and cousins, her own voice right in the middle of the bird-like cries as they rush from one devilment to another free as the wind. It was the sound she had heard before Eugene came. While she was growing up the house had been full of children and some of them always laughing or crying or just plain making noise. So while she prayed for a child to bless the love she shared with her man, she heard ringing in her ears, echoes of that houseful of children romping and squabbling. And while she waited for her son Eugene to return from the war, the same bittersweet echoes played in that emptiness only he could fill by coming home again. When the war was over,

when the news of V-J Day jiggled in a storm of static from the
radio and her man grabbed her by the waist and spun her till
they were both so dizzy he couldn't stand up any longer and
she collapsed giddily on the floor beside him, the whole world
was laughing, was grinning ear to ear and giggling like all the
kids on Bruston Hill did when they thought they had gotten
away with something, when they believed they were the smart-
est, slickest, prettiest things alive. But Eugene didn't come
back, and she waited for word of him and the weeks after V-
J Day turned into months and she did get word but didn't
believe the telegram from the War Office her man had carried
up the hill from the post office because that's the only way
mail got to the top of Bruston Hill, and the months became
years and she walked down the hill each morning to meet the
mailman as he made his rounds. On those walks down the steep
hill, rain or shine or snow or ice so bad you could hardly stand
up, on the walks to get a letter which would tell her the telegram
had been a mistake, that somebody had counted wrong, she'd
hear the noise of a houseful of children chirping and flying and
crashing into each other.

Always so many kids around it seemed like they came no
matter what, landing on the top of Bruston Hill like rain and
snow, like the change of seasons. To not have any when you
wanted one so bad and then to squeeze out only one and then
to lose that one on a beach six thousand miles from home when
there wasn't even a war anymore, none of that seemed right,
seemed possible. But that was her story. She was Bess and her
story had happened to her. You could ask anyone. Even short-
legged, moon-faced Aida could get that one right. One baby.
One boy child given and one taken away leaves none. No one.
Leaves Bess where she is on top of Bruston Hill where children
came thick and regular as flies or mosquitoes and grew like
weeds and made so much noise nobody could ever forget they
were around, could ever doubt the future since it would be
lifted and carried on all those brown shoulders in all those
brown bellies, on all those dirty brown feet scurrying around
busy all the time, knock you down if you not careful.

She heard them now. Wheeling above the trees. Swooping
and spiraling and dipping as if wings were no big thing, as if
anybody could grow them, as if darting through the empty air
were a trick as easy to learn as learning to wait for death.

Inside the house she tucked the slop jar back in its corner.

She brushed away a cobweb from her brow as she rose. Her hair was getting like that. Thin and wispy as what spiders spin in the corners of the house, dry as the skins of dust which floated everywhere when she got tired and didn't clean for a week. Once there had been more than enough hair to sit on. Long, thick hair all the way down her back. Of course he loved to brush it. And she'd let him. Fool loved to brush it best when he was drunk. Said it straightened out his head to stroke her long, soft hair and count the strokes and listen to it crackle in the winter. That man could put her to sleep brushing her hair. And more than once he'd passed out with the oak-backed brush clutched in his fist.

They all had that long, good hair. All her sisters. And they all breathed in whatever there was about Bruston Hill that made having babies easy as dancing. All of them but her. All but Bess who only got up on the ballroom floor once and did her number once and tripped and fell on her face before she could get back to her seat. Perhaps not always as easy as dancing. Some of the babies had come too early, some had been sickly and doomed, sometimes a spell of dryness, a winter of waiting and tears for this sister or that. Yet the hard times were never too hard. Of course you died a little but you couldn't stay dead because there was always that noisy mob to be fed and changed and yelled at when they knocked you off your feet or started tearing the house apart board by board. With that sound like the sea always in the background you couldn't stay dead long and your feet started to move in the rhythm of that sea song again so yes it had been as easy as dancing for all of them but her.

He would be Freeda's daughter Lizabeth's son. Freeda the quiet one raised by my sister Aida and Bill Campbell above the Fox Bar and Grill on Hamilton Avenue. Quiet as she was didn't stop her from running away with that gambling man John French. Quiet Freeda marrying a loud man twice as old as she was. Nineteen years between her and her man. Funny how things turn out. Gert had Freeda but Aida more like Freeda's mama. Aida raising Freeda while Gert gallivanting around. Then Lizabeth born dead. Freeda's first lying there blue as a piece of sky but May saved her. Little twist this way or that none them be here. They catch Mother Owens keep her down in slavery wouldn't be no Bruston Hill. Now Lizabeth's son out in my shed and he's too long, his feet stick out like they waiting for somebody to come chop them off so he'll fit. Laying there dead to the world as that wood stacked for winter. Just about all gone now. Had enough to get me through and now it's just scraps for the cooking stove and no more trips through the snow to keep the fire going. Now the ground soft under foot. Spring stink and summer stink worse to come.

Long straight hair she could sit on and he'd comb and comb, whistling sometimes the way he did, the blues he said, not the low down dirty or the lost my woman and gone or the good morning or good night blues but hair brushing blues he said when I asked him what he was whistling because I thought it sounded sad and maybe he was brushing my hair and thinking he had no son and wondering if it was me or if it was him or both of us together wrong when love don't bring nothing but those sighs and that sweat and everything getting weak and good but nothing else, nothing afterward inside me growing but love and love ain't a small thing but it ain't a son neither nor a little girl with long hair her mama can comb or her daddy when she hops on his knee and she's like a doll in his big hands combing and that's what I thought might be the sad part in what he was thinking when he whistled but he just said hair brushing blues and smiled at me and I let it be.

That's another thing she hear around here sometimes getting crazy as a coot on this hill she hear him whistling the blues the way he did a thousand years ago or whenever it was they lived together. Aida's man Bill Campbell could play that guitar named Corrinne he brought from down home, said it was full of letters from home and he would read them when he played and you'd listen and know just what he was talking about even though you never been South yourself, never down there where Bill Campbell and John French born but you'd understand the messages when Bill Campbell played them and then your man would pick them up and whistle them to nobody but you and that was how you got a home you never been to or never saw except in that music they made. Sometimes she'd hear him whistling and stop what she was doing and try to get closer. But if the sound came from outside by the trees it'd be gone before she could get there and if she was outside he'd always whistle those blues in the house and be gone before she could get the door open. Not the kind of sound that got louder when you got closer. The kind you have to stand still to hear. Still so nothing is moving inside, not your heart, your wind or your blood. You had to stop it all and stand in your tracks and you could hear it plain as day. But when the music got too good and you had to move something and started toward where it seemed to be coming from that movement killed it, chased it away. You never got closer. It just got farther away. But when it got so good you had to move, you had to move. Even though you chased it away every time. Even though you know you crazy in the first place to hear it and even crazier to believe you could get closer to wherever it is. Because he is dead and gone. Her man and all the blues he ever had are gone, gone, gone.

My sister Gert's great-grandson. Running from somebody, running from what he don't want to hear, from what has taken his eyes away and put two scared animals in his face.

It was his sister lost the baby. So many names, so many *great-grand* this and *in-law* that and cousins and names changing and changing again because getting married didn't mean a thing nowdays, getting married was just a way of confusing people and changing names like they was somebody new or somebody different and in a couple weeks the nigger out in the street chasing women again and all these silly girls got is a new name and babies and he's still having his fun. Then you hear about this one done broke up from that one and so and so is back together with whichamacallit and he's staying at his mama's now and her mama keeping the children. Don't none of it mean a thing. Ain't worth bothering about so she don't keep the names in her head. When she slows them down and looks into the faces like she's looking at snapshots then she puts it all together, follows the bloodlines which flow through her blood. The boy sleeping in her shed was a Lawson and his sister was Shirley, Lizabeth's middle child. She had seen the boy at the funeral when they buried Shirley's baby.

She said the words again to herself *buried Shirley's baby* and the words were what she had been avoiding all along since she saw the boy's face. But she couldn't help herself. Even if the words rocked the flimsy shack, rocked her soul as it plummeted with the crashing walls down toward the center of the earth. Sooner or later she'd put the faces together and say something like *buried Shirley's baby* and saying the words would be like hearing her man whistling the blues and knowing her first step toward him would crack the earth and knowing the crack was too high to get over and too wide to get around and too low to get under but knowing she can't help herself and moving anyway toward that sound, toward the emptiness which is all there is which is what she knows she will find after she has stepped toward him and the earth has swallowed him again, swallowed his hair brushing blues and all there is of him left to love. Those words she said to herself, couldn't help saying to herself *buried Shirley's baby* moved her off of Bruston Hill and down again into the Homewood streets where people were singing and crying and making love and losing children and changing names like names could make a difference, like any of it made a difference.

She stood back from the sink so the spigot's first sloppy burst wouldn't wet her housedress. The water coughed on like it always did, like somebody was trying to pour a whole bucketful at once through the fingertip-size hole, and the hole choked and spit water everywhere and after the bucketful exploded, just a trickle, red with rust at first, staining the chipped place next to the drain, then the blood color washed away as a steady slow trickle cleansed the pipes. She waited till the water cleared and she washed her hands. Water smelled like iron. Hands smelled like iron when she held them to her face and sniffed. Old iron a long time underground. Only thing good about the water was its meanness, its nastiness which cut the nastiness of Henry Bow's moonshine. Regular water just curdle up and die you pour in Bow's whiskey. If she had still been a Christian she would have thanked Jesus for the little bit of warm life in her hands this morning. She dried them on the dishtowel hanging beside the sink. Yes she would have thanked Jesus for the little bit of live juice in her joints this morning and thanked him for mean water that tames mean whiskey and thanked him for minding his own business and letting her mind hers without always having to be thanking Jesus.

Buried Shirley's baby,

She knew why she hated his long feet poking out of her shed. That boy's feet belonged down the hill, down in the Homewood streets and that's where they should have stayed because now she couldn't help herself, couldn't stop making the connections she knew she'd have to make. The last time she had seen him was down below in Homewood. She could hear his long feet shuffling up the aisle, hear them pause beside the casket in the silence of the chapel and then shuffle off again carrying the silence like dust so wherever he goes you can look down at his feet and know he's been standing beside death. She can hear his shuffle above the organ moan. He walks like a boy who had never heard music, who has never danced. His body ignores what the organ is playing, his body shies away from the funeral march the way the children shy away from her lips when their mothers bring them to kiss Mother Bess for good luck. She has a moustache now and her bottom lip is creased like the rim of a canyon. His skinny body hanging from his shoulders, wide shoulders like a clothesline with him hanging down thin as a sheet.

The child's dead. Everybody sad. But nobody wants to be here. Why they here then? Why they crying and paying Benson? Why all these big people sitting on these skimpy little chairs paying rent to Benson? Why that boy pretending he a man in a man's suit too big for him? Why he trying so hard to look like he ain't hearing nothing, seeing nothing, ain't never danced nor heard no music before?

Evil old woman thoughts. A crazy woman who watched an angel pick apart a cobweb stuck to the roof of the chapel. So intent on watching the angel she didn't hear the person next to her crying, didn't answer the question somebody asked her till whoever it was nudged her shoulder and said *Mother Bess, Mother Bess*. Perhaps she dreamed the little finicky angel. Only a cellophane-winged angel in a blue-eyed gown would have the patience to pick those dust threads apart one by one and wind each one up into a ball and tuck the balls into her blue-eyed gown without snapping one thread. Angels don't hurt things. Don't tear apart what other creatures have spent their precious time doing. Wasn't no point in ripping apart those little suncatching webs.

The dead child was . . . to her. Her sister's great-great-granddaughter was what to her. Lizabeth's girl Shirley had lost the baby laid out on the satin quilt. Was that why a crazy old woman from off the top of Bruston Hill sitting in Benson's Funeral Parlor? Because they came and got her. Because she let them. And if she snored while the others wept, if someone had to snap her out of her dreams *Mother Bess, Mother Bess* and chase away her angel, why did they want her, why did she let them bring her?

The boy would not let the music do anything to him. He ignored it as he shuffled up the aisle, weightless between his stiff shoulders and shoes. He was not in its gloom, his heart did not take its message and pump his blood in slow, weepy surges. He said it was not music. His hips, his hands refused it. Didn't even know what it was supposed to be. Up the aisle and pausing and looking up at the ceiling and nodding once quickly into the dark box. Did he shut his eyes or was it just the droop of his long lashes made his eyes look closed?

Then it was her turn and somebody mumbling *Mother Bess* and somebody taking her arm like she was a china cup and leading her from behind with pressure on her elbow like she was blind, like she couldn't see where she was going and needed somebody's busy fingers worrying her elbow like she was a baby taking its first steps and might fall and break into pieces all over Benson's chapel floor.

What she saw was white pillows and white fluff and a hole plunging through it all, a hole not stopping till it reached China or whatever there was if you dug as far as you could dig into the black earth. The baby's dark face like a hole in the white satin, a dark eye staring from the bottomless depths of the hole. The eye was the hole, the hole was a way of seeing the dark shaft. This child, this daughter of her sister's great-grand-daughter stared into a place an old woman could only glimpse as she rocked and rocked with both eyes pinched shut on the porch of the shack on Bruston Hill. This child staring forever, never blinking, beholding the darkness an old woman cannot bear for more than an instant before she turns away to lies.

Then she is being nudged again, steered again by whoever took that duty. You could trip over the thick music. The organ made the passage back to her seat treacherous because it moaned and dripped pain in slick pools over the floor. Nobody playing that music. It came from the mesh-faced box suspended in one corner of the ceiling. Nobody could play misery that long. If somebody felt bad as that organ sounded for as long as it groaned out its grief wouldn't nothing be left but a puddle of tears. Like the boy, she promised herself, she would never give in.

Back in her seat she swore she would never come down off Bruston Hill again. While the preacher spoke, she searched the ceiling for her angel. The angel was gone, but the cobweb she had picked apart had been made whole again closer to the chapel's three lean windows. Now it was not a veil but a beaded net to catch the light swimming through the colored glass.

She noticed for the first time the banks of flowers surround-

ing the casket, not because she saw them but because they
stank of spring. Preacher didn't talk very long. Couldn't be
much to say about a child. And this preacher didn't know how
to preach. Spoke like a white man. Nothing in him of old Frank
Felder. Reverend Felder be singing by now, have those glasses
pushed up on his bald head and mopping tears with that white
handkerchief big as a towel. His mouth be working like he's
trying to talk to somebody while he's singing, two conversa-
tions at once and everybody singing from their seats, singing
softer and slower as the verses of the hymn unravel, softer and
slower till the last verse is a whisper like they're trying to hear
what the old preacher is saying under his breath, hear what's
being said to him. She wished for rockers on the bottom of the
folding, funeral parlor chair. Old time music, old time preaching, the word not spoken but chanted. Loud in her, a tumult
and shout and tambourine rattle so full in her breast she wanted
to lay her head back and rock, rock, rock. Rock on home in
the dip and squeak of her comfortable chair. *Father along.*
Father along. She would take the baby on her lap and they'd
rock together because what else could you say what else could
you do when a life ain't even got started good yet and that life
gets taken away. They'd rock in the sunlight on the creaking
boards of that old porch and when the sun dropped out the sky
she'd hum the songs around the two of them like a blanket to
keep off the cold.

   She refused to go to the cemetery. She remembered that,
remembered three or four of them with their bushy heads together, talking like they did when they pretended like she wasn't
there. How every once in a while one of them would look up
quick from the busy huddle of talk and check to see if she was
still standing there and frown kind of disappointed she was.
She refused so one of the lean young men in a bright colored
suit had no business being worn to no funeral drove her back
up Bruston Hill. The last thing she remembered from that day
was the boy walking down Kelley Street. She saw him from
the window of the car and he was halfway down the block but
she could see he was still shuffling and see the pole jammed
across the shoulders of that man's suit too big for him to be
wearing. He was alone, moving away from the others as fast
as those stiff shoulders and man's suit and grave dust all over
his shoes would let him.

TOMMY

▼▼

It is happening again. He is watching it happen again. That killing day. Sees himself check out the Brass Rail. Can't see shit for a minute in the darkness. Just the juke box and beer smell and the stink from the men's room door always hanging open. Uncle Carl ain't there yet. Must be his methadone day. Carl with his bad feet like he's in slow motion wants to lay them dogs down easy as he can on the hot sidewalk. Little sissy walking on eggs steps pussy-footing up Frankstown to the clinic. Uncle Carl ain't treating to no beer to start the day so he backs out into the brightness of the Avenue, to the early afternoon street quiet after the blast of nigger music and nigger talk.

Ain't nothing to it. Nothing. If he goes left under the trestle and up the stone steps or ducks up the bare path worn through the weeds on the hillside he can walk along the tracks to the park. Early for the park. The sun everywhere now giving the grass a yellow sheen. If he goes right it's down the Avenue to where the supermarkets and Murphy's 5&10 used to be. Man, they sure did fuck with this place. What he thinks each time he stares at what was once the heart of Homewood. Nothing. A parking lot and empty parking stalls with busted meters. Only a fool leave his car next to one of the bent meter poles. Places to park so you can shop in stores that ain't there no more. Remembers his little Saturday morning wagon hustle when him and all the other kids would lay outside the A&P to haul groceries. Still some white ladies in those days come down from Thomas Boulevard to shop and if you're lucky get one of them and get tipped a quarter. Some of them fat black bitches be in church every Sunday have you pulling ten tons of rice and beans all the way to West Hell and be smiling and yakking all the way and saying What a nice boy you are and

55

I knowed your mama when she was little and please sonny just
set them inside on the table and still be smiling at you with
some warm glass of water and a dime after you done hauled
their shit halfway round the world.

Hot in the street but nobody didn't like you just coming in
and sitting in their air conditioning unless you buy a drink and
set it in front of you. The pool room hot. And too early to be
messing with those fools on the corner. Always somebody
trying to hustle. Man, when you gonna give me my money,
man, I been waiting too long for my money, man, lemme hold
this quarter till tonight, man. I'm getting over tonight, man.
And the buses climbing the hill and turning the corner by the
state store and fools parked in the middle of the street and
niggers getting hot honking to get by and niggers paying them
no mind like they got important business and just gon sit there
blocking traffic as long as they please and the buses growling
and farting those fumes when they struggle around the corner.

Look to the right and to the left but ain't nothing to it,
nothing saying move one way or the other. Homewood Avenue
a darker grey channel between the grey sidewalks. Tar patches
in the asphalt. Looks like somebody's bad head with the ring-
worm. Along the curb ground glass sparkles below the broken
neck of a Tokay bottle. Just the long neck and shoulders of the
bottle and a piece of label hanging. Somebody should make
a deep ditch out of Homewood Avenue and just go on and push
the row houses and boarded storefronts into the hole. Bury it
all, like in a movie he had seen a dam burst and the flood
waters ripping through the dry bed of a river till the roaring
water overflowed the banks and swept away trees and houses,
uprooting everything in its path like a cleansing wind.

He sees Homewood Avenue dipping and twisting at Hamilton. Where Homewood crests at Frankstown the heat is a
shimmering curtain above the trolley tracks. No trolleys anymore. But somebody forgot to take up the tracks and pull down
the cables. So when it rains or snows some fool always gets
caught and the slick tracks flip a car into a telephone pole or
upside a hydrant and the cars just lay there with crumpled
fenders and windshields shattered, laying there for no reason
just like the tracks and wires are there for no reason now that
buses run where the 88 and the 82 Lincoln trolleys used to go.

He remembers running down Lemington Hill because the

trolleys only came once an hour after midnight and if he misses
an 82 it will mean an hour on the windy corner. He thinks he
can hear the clatter of the trolley starting its long glide down
Lincoln Avenue. The Dells still working out on *Why Do You
Have To Go* and the tip of his dick wet and his balls aching
and his finger sticky but he forgets all that and forgets the half
hour in Sylvia's hallway because he is flying now, all long
strides and pumping arms and his fists opening and closing on
the night air as he grapples for balance in a headlong rush down
the steep hill. He can hear the trolley coming and wishes he
was a bird soaring through the black night, a bird with shiny
chrome fenders and fishtails and a Continental kit. He tries to
watch his feet, avoid the cracks and gulleys in the sidewalk.
He can hear the trolley's bell and crash of its steel wheels
against the tracks. He was all in Sylvia's drawers and she was
wet as a dishrag and moaning her hot breath into his ears and
the record player inside the door hiccupped for the thousandth
time caught in the groove of grey noise at the end of the disc.

He remembers and curses again the empty trolley screaming
past him as he froze half a block from the corner. Honky driver
half sleep in his yellow bubble. As the trolley lurched past the
bottom of the hill, a red spark popped above its gimpy antenna.
Chick had his nose open and his dick hard but he should have
been cool, been out of there and down the hill because it was
too late now. Nothing for it now but to walk. He had to walk
that night and in the darkness over his head the cables swayed
and sang long after the trolley had disappeared. He had to walk
cause that's all there was to it. And still no ride of his own so
he's still walking. Nothing to it. Either right or left, either up
Homewood or down Homewood, walking his hip walk, making
something out of the way he is walking since there is nothing
else to do, no place to go so he makes something of the going,
lets them see him moving in his own down way, his stylized
walk which nobody could walk better if they had some place
to go.

Thinking of a chump shot on the nine ball which he blew
and cost him a quarter for the game and his last dollar on a
side bet. Of pulling on his checkered bells that morning and
the black tank top. How the creases were dead and grape pop
or something on the front and a million wrinkles behind the
knees and where his thighs came together. Junkie, wino-look-

ing pants he would have rather died than wear just a few years
ago when he was one of the cleanest cats in Westinghouse High
School. Sharp and leading the Commodores. Doo Wah Diddy,
Wah Diddy Bop. Thirty-five dollar pants when most the cats
in the House couldn't spend that much for a suit. It was a bitch
in the world. Stone bitch. Feeling like Mister Tooth Decay
crawling all sweaty out of the grey sheets. Mama could wash
them everyday, they still be grey. Like his underclothes. Like
every motherfucking thing they had and would ever have. Doo
Wah Daddy. The rake jerked three or four times through his
bush. Left there as decoration and weapon. You could fuck up
a cat with those steel teeth. You could get the points sharp as
needles. And draw it swift as Billy the Kid.

Thinking it be a bitch out here. Niggers write all over everything don't even know how to spell. Drawing power fists look
like a loaf of bread.

Thinking this whole Avenue is like somebody's mouth they
let some jive dentist fuck with. All these old houses nothing
but rotten teeth and these raggedy pits is where some been dug
out or knocked out and ain't nothing left but stumps and snag-
gle-teeth just waiting to go. Thinking, that's right. That's just
what it is. Why it stinks around here and why ain't nothing but
filth and germs and rot. And what that make me? What it make
all these niggers? Thinking yes, yes, that's all it is.

Mr. Strayhorn where he always is down from the corner of
Hamilton and Homewood sitting on a folding chair beside his
ice-ball cart. A sweating canvas draped over the front of the
cart to keep off the sun. Somebody said the old man a hundred
years old, somebody said he was a bad dude in his day. A
gambler like his own Granddaddy John French had been. They
say Strayhorn whipped three cats half to death try to cheat him
in the alley behind Dumferline. Took a knife off one and
whipped all three with his bare hands. Just sits there all summer
selling ice balls. Old and can hardly see. But nobody don't
bother him even though he got this pockets full of change every
evening.

Shit. One of the young boys will off him one night. Those
kids was stone crazy. Kill you for a dime and think nothing
of it. Shit. Rep don't mean a thing. They come at you in packs.
Like wild dogs. Couldn't tell those young bloods nothing. He
thought he had come up mean. Thought his running buddies

be some terrible dudes. Shit. These kids coming up been into
more stuff before they twelve than most grown men do they
whole lives.

Hard out here. He stares into the dead storefronts. Sometimes
they get in one of them. Take it over till they get run out or
set it on fire or it get so filled with shit and nigger piss don't
nobody want to use it no more except for winos and junkies
come in at night and could be sleeping on a bed of nails wouldn't
make no nevermind to those cats. He peeks without stopping
between the wooden slats where the glass used to be. Like he
is reading the posters, like there might be something he needed
to know on these faded pieces of cardboard. Like he might find
out why he's twenty-five years old and never had nothing and
never will. Like they might be selling a pill bring Sonny back
and Sarah back and everything happy ever after.

Self-defense demonstration. Ahmed Jamal at the Syria
Mosque. Rummage Sale. Omega Boat Ride in August. The Dells
coming to the Diamond Roller Rink. Madame Walker's Beauty
Products.

A dead bird crushed dry and paper thin in the alley between
Albion and Tioga. Like somebody had smeared it with tar and
mashed it between the pages of a giant book. If you hadn't
seen it in the first place, still plump and bird colored, you'd
never recognize it now. Looked like the lost sole of somebody's
shoe. He had watched it happen. Four or five days was all it
took. On the third day he thought a cat had dragged it off. But
when he passed the corner next afternoon he found the dark
shape in the grass at the edge of the cobblestones. The head
was gone and the yellow smear of beak but he recognized the
rest. By then already looking like the raggedy sole somebody
had walked off their shoe.

He was afraid of anything dead. He could look at something
dead but no way was he going to touch it. Didn't matter, big
or small, he wasn't about to put his hands near nothing dead.
His daddy had whipped him when his mother said he sassed
her and wouldn't take the dead rat out of the trap. He could
whip him again but no way he was gon touch nothing dead.
The dudes come back from Nam talk about puddles of guts and
scraping parts of people into plastic bags. They talk about
carrying their own bag so they could get stuffed in if they got
wasted. Have to court-martial his ass. No way he be carrying

no body bag. Felt funny now carrying out the big green bags
you put your garbage in. Any kind of plastic sack and he's
thinking of machine guns and dudes screaming and grabbing
their bellies and rolling around like they do when they're hit
in Iwo Jima and Tarawa or The Dirty Dozen or The Magnificent
Seven or The High Plains Drifter, but the screaming is not in
the darkness on a screen it is bright, green afternoon and Willie
Thompson and them are on patrol. It is a street like Homewood.
Quiet like Homewood this time of day and bombed out like
Homewood is. Just pieces of buildings standing here and there
and fire scars and places ripped and kicked down and cars
stripped and dead at the curb. They are moving along in single
file and their uniforms are hip and their walks are hip and they
are kind of smiling and rubbing their weapons and cats passing
a joint fat as a cigar down the line. You can almost hear music
from where Porgy's Record Shop used to be, like the music
so fine it's still there clinging to the boards, the broken glass
on the floor, the shelves covered with roach shit and rat shit,
a ghost of the music rifting sweet and mellow like the smell
of home cooking as the patrol slips on past where Porgy's used
to be. Then...

Rat Tat Tat...Rat Tat Tat...Ra Ta Ta Ta Ta Ta Ta...

Sudden but almost on the beat. Close enough to the beat
so it seems the point man can't take it any longer, can't play
this soldier game no longer and he gets happy and the smoke
is gone clear to his head so he jumps out almost on the beat,
wiggling his hips and throwing up his arms so he can get it all,
go on and get down. Like he is exploding to the music. To the
beat which pushes him out there all alone, doing it, and it is
Rat Tat Tat and we all want to fingerpop behind his twitching
hips and his arms flung out but he is screaming and down in
the dirty street and the street is exploding all around him in
little volcanoes of dust. And some of the others in the front of
the patrol go down with him. No rhythm now, just stumbling,
or airborne like their feet jerked out from under them. The
whole hip procession buckling, shattered as lines of deadly
force stitch up and down the Avenue.

Hey man, what's to it? Ain't nothing to it man you got it
baby hey now where's it at you got it you got it ain't nothing
to it something to it I wouldn't be out here in all this sun you
looking good you into something go on man you got it all you

know you the Man hey now that was a stone fox you know what I'm talking about you don't be creeping past me yeah nice going you got it all save some for me Mister Clean you seen Ruchell and them yeah you know how that shit is the cat walked right on by like he ain't seen nobody but you know how he is get a little something don't know nobody shit like I tried to tell the cat get straight nigger be yourself before you be by yourself you got a hard head man hard as stone but he ain't gon listen to me shit no can't nobody do nothing for the cat less he's ready to do for hisself Ruchell yeah man Ruchell and then come by here little while ago yeah baby you got it yeah lemme hold this little something I know you got it you the Man you got to have it lemme hold a little something till this evening man I'll put you straight tonight man you know your man do you right I unnerstand yeah that's all that's to it nothing to it I'ma see you straight man yeah you fall on by the crib yeah we be into something tonight you fall on by.

Back to the left now. Up Hamilton, past the old man who seems to sleep beside his cart until you get close and then his yellow eyes under the straw hat brim follow you. Cut through the alley past the old grade school. Halfway up the hill the game has already started. You have been hearing the basketball patted against the concrete, the hollow thump of the ball glancing off the metal backboards. Ball players half-naked out there under that hot sun, working harder than niggers ever did picking cotton. They shine. They glide and leap and fly at each other like their dark bodies are at the ends of invisible strings. This time of day the court is hot as fire. Burn through your shoes. Maybe that's why the niggers play like they do, running and jumping so much because the ground's too hot to stand on. His brother used to play here all day. Up and down all day in the hot sun with the rest of the crazy ball players. Old dudes and young dudes and when people on the side waiting for winners they'd get to arguing and you could hear them bad-mouthing all the way up the hill and cross the tracks in the park. Wolfing like they ready to kill each other.

His brother one of the old dudes now. Still crazy about the game. He sees a dude lose his man and fire a jumper from the side. A double pump, a lean, and the ball arched so it kisses the board and drops through the iron. He could have played the game. Tall and loose. Hands bigger than his brother's.

Could palm a ball when he was eleven. Looks at his long
fingers. His long feet in raggedy-ass shoes. The sidewalk sloped
and split. Little plots of gravel and weeds where whole paving
blocks torn away. Past the dry swimming pool. Just a big
concrete hole now where people piss and throw bottles like you
got two points for shooting them in. What's left of a backstop
dropping like a rusty spiderweb from tall metal poles, and
beyond the flaking mesh of the screen the dusty field and
beyond that a jungle of sooty trees below the railroad tracks.
They called it the Bums' Forest when they were kids and
bombed the winos sleeping down there in the shade of the
trees. If they walked the tracks all the way to the park they'd
have to cross the bridge over Homewood Avenue. Hardly room
for the trains on the bridge so they always ran and some fool
always yelling *Train's coming* and everybody else yells and
then it's your chest all full and your heart pumping to keep up
with the rest. Because the train couldn't kill everybody. It
might get the last one, the slow one, but it wouldn't run down
all the crazy niggers screaming and hauling ass over Homewood
Avenue.

From the track, you could look down on the winos curled
up under a tree or sitting in a circle sipping from bottles wrapped
in brown paper bags. At night they would have fires, hot as
it was some nights you'd still see their fires when you sat in
the bleachers watching the Legion team kick butt. From high
up on the tracks you could bomb the Bums' Forest. Stones
hissed through the thick leaves. Once in a while a lucky shot
shattered a bottle. Some grey, sorry-assed wino motherfucker
waking up and shaking his fist and cussing at you and some
fool yells *He's coming, he's coming*.

He had heard stories about the old days when all the men
used to hang out in the woods below the tracks. Gambling and
drinking wine and telling lies and singing those old time, down
home songs. Hang out there in the summer and when it got
cold they'd loaf in the Bucket of Blood on the corner of Frankstown and Tioga. His granddaddy was in the stories, old John
French one of the baddest dudes ever walked these Homewood
streets. Old, big-hat John French. They said his granddaddy
could sing up a storm and now his jitterbug father up in the
choir of Homewood A.M.E. Zion, next to Mrs. So and So
who hit those high notes. Sound almost like Reba Love Jackson.
He was his daddy's son, people said. When he was singing

regular, when he was tenor lead of the Commodores and they'd git round a bench and get down. Everybody knew the Commodores was the baddest group. If that cat hadn't fucked us over with the record we might have made the big time. Achmet backing us on the conga. Tito on bongos. Tear up the park. Commodores used to stone tear it up. Under the trees and the little kids and old folks all gone home and ain't nobody in the park but who supposed to be and you got your old lady on the side listening or maybe you singing pretty, trying to pull some fine bitch catch your eye in the crowd. Those were good days, real good days when everything got swift and mellow and fine. The drums, the smoke, the sun like fire in those big trees and you out there flying and the Commodores steady taking care of business behind your tenor lead.

You got to go to church. I'm not asking I'm telling. Now you get those shoes shined and I don't want to hear another word out you, young man. She is ironing his Sunday shirt hot and stiff. She hums along with the gospel songs on the radio. *Don't make me send you to your father.* Who is in the bathroom for the half hour he takes doing whatever to get hisself together. Making everybody else late. Singing in there while he shaves. You don't want to be the next one after him. *You got five minutes, boy. Five minutes and your teeth better be clean and your hands and face shining.* Gagging in the funky bathroom, not wanting to take a breath. How you supposed to brush your teeth, the cat just shit in there. *You're going to church this week and every week. This is my time and don't you try and spoil it, boy. Don't you get no attitude and try to spoil church for me.* He is in the park now, sweating in the heat, a man now, a father himself now but he can hear his mother's voice plain as day, filling up all the empty space around him just as it did in the house on Finance Street. She'd talk them all to church every Sunday. Use her voice like a club to beat everybody out the house.

His last time in church was a Thursday. They had up the scaffolding to clean the ceiling and Deacon Barclay's truck was parked outside. Barclay's Hauling, Cleaning and General Repairing. Young People's Gospel Chorus had practice on Thursdays and he knew Adelaide would be there. That chick looked good even in them baggy choir robes. He had seen her on Sunday because his mama cried and asked him to go to church.

Because she knew he stole the money out her purse but he had lied and said he didn't and she knew he was feeling guilty and knew he'd go to church to make up to her. Adelaide up there with the Young People's Gospel Chorus rocking church. Rocking church and he'd go right on up there, the lead of the Commodores, and sing gospel with them if he could get next to that fine Adelaide. So Thursday he left the poolroom, *Where you tipping off to, Man? None of your motherfucking business, motherfucker*, about seven when she had choir practice and look here Adelaide I been digging you for a long time. I been knowing you for years girl, since your mama brought you in here and you wasn't nothing but a little thing in pigtails. Yeah I been digging on you a long time. Longer and deeper than you'll ever know. Let me tell you something. I know what you're thinking, but don't say it, don't break my heart by saying you heard I was a jive cat and nothing to me and stay away from him he's married and got a baby and he ain't no good and stuff like that I know I got a rep that way but you grown enough now to know how people talk and how you got to find things out for yourself. Don't be putting me down till you let me have a little chance to speak for myself. I ain't gon lie now. I been out here in the world and into some jive tips. Yeah, I did my time diddy boppin and trying my wheels out here in the street. I was a devil. I got into everything I was big and bad enough to try. Look here. I could write the book. Pimptime and partytime and jive to stay alive, but I been through all that and that ain't what I want. I want something special, something solid. A woman, not no fingerpopping young girl got her nose open and her behind wagging all the time. That's right. That's right, I ain't talking nasty, I'm talking what I know. I'm talking truth tonight and listen here I been digging you all these years and waiting for you because all that Doo Wah Diddy ain't nothing, you hear, nothing to it. You grown now and I need just what you got...

Thursday rapping in the vestibule with Adelaide was the last time in Homewood A.M.E. Zion Church. Had to be swift and clean. Swoop down like a hawk and get to her mind. Tuesday she still crying and gripping the elastic of her drawers and saying no. Next Thursday the only singing she doing is behind some bushes in the park. *Oh, Baby. Oh, Baby, it's so good*. Tore that pussy up.

Don't make no difference. No big thing. She giving it to

somebody else now. All that good stuff still shaking under her robe every second Sunday when the Young People's Gospel Chorus in the loft beside the pulpit. Old man Barclay like he guarding the church door asked me did I come around to help clean.

Mr. Barclay, I wish I could help but I'm working nights. Matter of fact I'm a little late now. I'm gon be here on my night off, though.

He knew I was lying. Old bald dude standing there in his coveralls and holding a bucket of Lysol and a scrub brush. Worked all his life and got a piece of truck and a piece of house and still running around yes sirring and no mamming the white folks and cleaning their toilets. And he's doing better than most of these chumps. Knew I was lying but smiled his little smile cause he knows my mama and knows she's a good woman and knows Adelaide's grandmother and knows if I ain't here to clean he better guard the door with his soap and rags till I go on about my business.

Ruchell and them over on the bench. Niggers is high already. They ain't hardly out there in the sun bar–b–queing their brains less they been into something already. Niggers be hugging the shade till evening less they been into something.

Hey now.

What's to it, Tom?

You cats been into something.

You ain't just talking.

Ruchell man, we got that business to take care of.

Stone business, man. I'm stone ready to T.C.B.

You ain't ready for nothing, nigger.

Hey man, we gon get it together. I'm ready, man I ain't never been so ready. We gon score big, Brother Man.

The reason it's gon work is the white boy is greedy. He's so greedy he can't stand for the nigger to have nothing. Did you see Indovina's eyes when we told him we had copped a truckload of color TVs? Shit man. I could hear his mind working. Calculating like. These niggers is dumb. I can rob these niggers. Click. Click. Clickedy. Rob the shit out of these dumb spooks. They been robbing us so long they think that's the way things supposed to be. They so greedy their hands get sweaty they see a nigger with something worth stealing.

So he said he'd meet us at the car lot.

That's the deal. I told him we had two vans full.

And Ricky said he'd let you use his van.

I already got the keys, man. I told you we were straight with Ricky. He ain't even in town till the weekend.

I drive up then and you hide in the back.

Yeah dude. Just like we done said a hundred times. You go in the office to make the deal and you know how Indovina is. He's gon send out his nigger Chubby to check the goods.

And you jump Chubby.

Be on him like white on rice. Freeze that nigger till you get the money from Indovina.

You sure Indovina ain't gon try and follow us?

Shit, man. He be happy to see us split...

With his money.

Indovina gon do whatever you say. Just wave your piece in his face a couple of times. That fat ofay motherfucker ain't got no heart. Chubby is his heart and Ruchell stone take care of Chubby.

I still think Indovina might go to the cops. And I ain't gon back to no slammer. One year in the motherfucker like to drove me crazy, man and I ain't takin no chances. Have to kill me to get me in a cage again.

Ain't nobody gon no jail. What Indovina be tellin some cops? What he gon say? He was trying to buy some hot tee vees and got ripped off? He ain't hardly saying that. He might say he got robbed and try to collect insurance. He's slick like that. But if he goes to the cops you can believe he won't be describing us. Naw. The pigs know that greasy dago is a crook. Everybody knows it and won't be no problem. Just score and blow. Score and blow. Leave this motherfucking sorry ass town. Score and blow.

At the stoplight he stares at the big sign hanging over the Boulevard. A smiling Duquesne Pilsner Duke with his glass of beer. The time and temperature flash beneath the Duke's uniformed chest. Ricky had installed a tape deck in the dash. A tangle of wires drooped from its guts, but the sound was good. One speaker for the cab, another for the back where Ruchell was sitting on the roll of carpet Ricky had back there. Al Green: *Call Me*. Ricky could do things. He made his own tapes; he was customizing the delivery van. Next summer Ricky driving to California. Fixing up the van so he could live in it. The dude was good with his hands. He had been a mechanic in the war. Government paid him for the shattered knee. Ricky said, Got me a new knee now. Got a four-wheeled knee that's gonna ride me away from all this mess. Disability money paid for the van, the customizing, the stereo tape deck. Ricky would always have that limp, but the cat was getting hisself together.

Flags were strung across the entrance to the used car lot. Wind got them popping and dancing. Rows and rows of cars all looking clean and new under the lights. He parked on the street, in the deep shadow at the far end of Indovina's glowing corner. He sees them through the office window. Indovina and his nigger.

Hey, Chubby.

What's happening now? Chubby had shoulders wide as the door. He was Indovina's nigger all the way. Had his head laid back so far on his neck it's like he's looking at you through his noseholes instead of his eyes.

You got the merchandise?

You got my money?

Ain't your money yet. I thought you said two vans full.

Can't drive but one at a time. My partner's at a phone booth right now. Got the number here. You show me the bread and he bring the rest.

I want to see them all before I give you a penny. Indovina drums the desk top. His fingers are hairy. Look like they itch him.

Look, Mr. Indovina. This ain't no bullshit tip. We got the stuff, alright. Good stuff like I said. Sony portables. All the same . . . still in the boxes.

Let's go look.

I want to see some bread first.

Give Chubby your key. Chubby, check it out. Count them. Make sure the cartons ain't broke open.

I want to see some bread.

Bread. Bread. My cousin DeLuca runs a bakery. I don't deal with *bread*. I got money. See. That's money in my hand. I got plenty cash money buy your television sets buy your van buy you.

Just trying to do square business, Mr. Indovina.

Don't forget to check the cartons. Make sure they're sealed.

*   *   *

Somebody must be down. Ruchell or Chubby down. He
had heard two shots. He sees himself in the plate glass window.
In a fishbowl and patches of light gliding past. Except where
the floodlights are trained the darkness outside is impenetrable.
He cannot see past his image in the glass.

Turn out the goddamn lights.

You kill me you be sorry . . . kill me you be real sorry . . .
if one of them dead out there it's just one nigger kill another
nigger . . . you kill me you be sorry . . . you killing a white man.

Tommy's knee skids on the desk and he slams the gun across
the man's fat, sweating face with all the force of his lunge. He
is stumbling over the desk, scattering paper and junk, looking
down at Indovina's white shirt, his hairy arms folded over his
head. He is thinking of the shots. Thinking that everything is
wrong, the lights, the shots, the white man cringing on the
floor behind the steel desk. Him atop the desk, his back exposed
to anybody coming through the glass door.

Then he is running. Flying into the darkness. He is crouching
so low he loses his balance and trips onto all fours. The gun
leaps from his hand and skitters towards a wall of tires. He
hears the pennants crackling. Hears a motor starting and Ruchell calling his name.

What you mean you didn't get the money? Shit, man. I
done wasted Chubby and you didn't even get the money. Aw,
shit. Shit. Shit.

He had nearly tripped again over the man's body. Without
knowing how he knew, he knew Chubby was dead. Dead as
the sole of his shoe. He should stop; he should try to help. But
the body was lifeless. He couldn't touch . . .

Ruchell is shuddering and crying. Tears glazing his eyes
and he wonders if Ruchell can see where he's going, if Ruchell
knows he is driving like a wild man on both sides of the street
and weaving in and out the line of traffic. Horns blare after
them. Then it's Al Green up again. He didn't know how, when
or who pushed the button but it was Al Green blasting in the
cab. *Help me Help me Help me . . .*

Jesus is waiting

And Ruchell crying like a baby and shaking all over Ruchell
is clutching the wheel the way Sonny would hang on to the

edge of his crib, when he woke up in the middle of the night soaking wet and wailing for somebody to come get him. *Help me Help me.* He snatches at the tape deck with both hands to turn it down or off or rip the goddamn cartridge from the machine.

Slow down, man. Slow down. You gon get us stopped.

Rolling down his window. The night air sharp in his face. The whirr of tape dying then a hum of silence. The traffic sounds and city sounds pressing again into the cab.

CLEMENT

▼▼▼

Clement thinks about roller skates. Skates make his job easier. Be skating up and down Homewood Avenue. Be up and out Big Bob's and the Brass Rail and Miss Claudine's and the cleaners and the drugstore so fast nobody see him coming and going. Like lightning. Captain Lightning on his red skates with silver wheels and silver wings so fast he be back before they know he gone. Speedo. Zip. Zap. Won't see nothing but a blur. Captain Blur. Captain Flash when he come streaking down off Bruston Hill. Look out. Here he come. Zoooom. Them skates be tearing up that hill. Them skates be breaking his ass with all them holes in the streets. Homewood ain't no place for nothing got wheels. Bust up your ride. Bust you up you fool nough come rolling down Bruston Hill. Captain Broke Butt. Captain Bandage Ass. You want see Clement you got to go to the hospital. Clement ain't doing his job. Laid up in bed. Big Bob go for his own warm milk and Miss Claudine don't speak. Act like she ain't never seen him before and he drink all that poison and she say, Carry him out please, Mister Lavender. Take his blubber butt on out here.

No. Clement ain't been round. Big Bob's got hair to the ceiling. Can't get the door open no more. Bell don't ring. Nothing. Like a jungle full of Brillo in there.

Miss Bess said come tomorrow afternoon. He can hear her plain as day. Her voice calling down off that mountain and it be like she standing right there talking in his ear. Some oleo. Some milk. Three pound potatoes. Yellow onions. Don't even have to go up and ask. Know just what she want sometimes and carry it up there. But she's calling and ain't nothing he can do. Captain Band-Aid strapped down in that hospital bed and he hears her but he stone out of business. Them skates still flying down Bruston but he ain't on top. His riding days done.

70

You hold on, Miss Bess.

Maybe she send down the ghost. Maybe she give him one those shopping bags send him down here. Big Bob say he better not stop. Better keep running and never look back. Big Bob say they gon make him example. Say two dead niggers in one day embarrassing. Maybe they leave him alone till he get them groceries for Miss Bess. Maybe they see he ain't looking for no trouble. Maybe they see he a ghost already.

Big Bob turns on the TV for six o'clock news. Just news and ball games on Big Bob's TV. None the rest of that mess worth a good goddamn he say. Insultin to his intelligence he say. He turns on the news then opens his evening paper. Can't tell if he's watching or reading. *Both* he say if you fool enough to ask. *Both* and mind your own damned business cain't you see I'm busy minding mine.

Clement's business running errands. Clement's business keep this place clean. And listening for Mother Bess. He listens. But she said tomorrow afternoon. She call tomorrow. If that ghost don't take his job.

TOMMY

▼▼

Someone pulling on his foot. Have him by the foot and dragging
him out the cave where he's been hiding. A deep, dark, warm
cave. A cave as black and secret as his blood. Yes. He is hiding
deep in the rivers of his blood, in a subterranean chamber where
his own blood is gathered in a still, quiet pool. But they have
him by the foot dragging him out. He feels himself sliding,
slipping, and he tries to hold on with both his hands but the
walls are slick as ice cream, raw as meat. He can't get a
handhold. He struggles but he can't hold on. His arms are
flailing but he doesn't know how to swim so he is just flapping
and flailing and beating his own blood as they drag him out.
He wants to scream but he doesn't want to wake anybody up.
If he wakes anyone up they'll just help the others pull. So he
shouts no no no as loud as he can but inside so no one can
hear. Splashing his own blood against the walls of the tunnel.
Then the *no*'s are please are please please please like James
Brown in the song as light cracks the ceiling and floods in a
cresting wave, choking, surging, putting out his eyes if he
opens them, welding them shut forever if he doesn't.

Wake up. Wake up now. She is tapping his foot with a
stick. That evil old woman. He is lying in shadow and she is
above him staring down on him, the sunlight aflame on her
shoulder. He looks past her burning flesh into the tops of the
trees which filter the shafts of sunlight. Blinking in the sudden
glare he can see through her, past her, she is a ghost quivering
without meat or bone and he can see through her to the dark
tree trunks, to the tip of the hill to the burnished haze hanging
over the city.

Come on you. Wake up, you. It's getting close to dark and
I want you away from here. The sun going down and I want
your feet beating a path away from my door.

She steps closer to his face. She taps the stick harder now, not against the sole of his shoe now but harder now, a rat tat tat drumming against a log he had rolled from the shed to make room for himself. She was solid again, black and grey and brown, the lines of her face, the shape of her body sharply etched against the sky. Behind her, below her the city flamed.

Wake up, you. Sun's setting and least I can do is give you a cup of soup. You my sister's great-grandson and that's the best I can do before I send you on your way.

The drumming is inside his head. Her stick tapping against the log as loud as the *no*'s he had been screaming. Had she been pulling his foot? In the dream the grip on his ankle had been as tight, as heavy as a leg iron. This frail old woman didn't have that kind of strength left in her hands, nowhere in her body. But the stick chopped at the log like an ax. If she hit his foot the way she hit the wood she'd shatter his bones.

Hey, Mother Bess. Just gimme a minute to get myself together. That's what he wanted to say but he knew his words were jumbled, were just noise and all she'd hear were grunts and groans.

He sits up and bumps his head on something. A shelf, a two by four, a beam, something solid and wooden cracks him as he tries to straighten up into a sitting position. He rolls away from the blow and the scabs on his elbows and knee split but he keeps moving till he scrambles to his feet. Feet somebody had chained. Feet somebody had hold of dragging him down to hell.

You a sight. You sure are a sight.

He brushes at dirt and wood shavings and sawdust and leaves. The ground had been damp and his body was stiff.

Look at you. Ain't you a sight. Like something the cat drag in.

I'm in trouble, Mother Bess.

Any fool see that. But I don't want to hear about your trouble. I'ma feed you cause you my sister Gert's great-grandson. Cause I seen your mama, Lizabeth, the minute after she born. Prayed for you and your brothers and sister each time I heard Lizabeth had a baby on the way. Prayed if I was still praying at the time and if I wasn't praying I was hoping for the best for all youall because your mama Lizabeth was my sister's grandchild. So I'ma feed you and get you out of here as soon as it's dark but I don't want to hear none your troubles.

He watched her walk to the shack. She used the knobby stick like a cane to pick her way over the rutted ground. But the stick wasn't a cane because she didn't lean on it. The stick was more like those rods witches use to find water, or like those poles soldiers stick in the ground to find their way through a mine field. Because that's how she used it. Poking it slowly into the ground, picking, sorting, testing the broken earth as if parts of it were unfit, unsafe, as if she could take nothing for granted so she had to piece together slowly, cautiously, a path from the shed to the shack. He remembered being little and squatting down to watch ants cross the handfuls of dirt he'd throw in their way. Sometimes they darted over the barricade but sometimes they measured each step, rearing up on their back legs, probing with their antennas, pawing and peering side to side. That's how she crossed the yard. And the bowlegged stick wasn't a cane but like those long feelers jutting from the ants' faces.

Soon as he got to his feet he knew he was going to puke. He forced himself step by step till he stood where he had been standing that morning or a hundred mornings ago, whenever it was because once sleep came it had been like dying and now he had no way of telling whether hours had passed or days or a lifetime. Was the sun sinking over there beyond the invisible rivers the same sun he had watched rising on Bruston Hill just that morning? Did this fall go with that rise, or had there been a million years separating them, a million years and the sun bouncing like a basketball up and down, up and down so many times nobody cared or could tell the difference? And the thought of the sun rising and falling faster than his heartbeat, the thought of years rushing by too fast to count them, the thought of all the days of his life gone faster than even that, lost to him, gone gone gone and leaving nothing behind but the sour taste in his mouth and the swelling emptiness in his belly, all those thoughts brought the nastiness rushing to his throat and he puked down over the edge of the world, down into the molten sprawl of the city.

The last strength went out of him and he dropped to his knees so he wouldn't topple over the sheer edge of Bruston Hill, topple and fall forever, fall and bounce and split and tumble and unravel till he splashed in the rivers at the city's heart. Not much in his stomach to bring up but the shudders kept coming. Whole body wanted to turn itself inside out and jump through his throat. His spit was thick with mucus when he wiped the drool from his chin and tongued out the inside of his mouth. He stared at the little glistening puddle under the trees. Hardly a cupful. Felt like a herd of elephants stampeding in his stomach and now it just sat there mocking him. He wondered if the old woman had been watching. If she had seen him double over and fall to his knees, shaking and whining like a sick puppy. This was her place, her yard, she was the caretaker of these ruins at the top of Bruston Hill. He wanted to bury the vomit, scrub the carpet of grassy stubble. On his feet again he looked toward the house but the slanting overhang of the back porch darkened the window and he couldn't see through it, couldn't catch any sign of life, couldn't find her face and say he was sorry. Wouldn't say that anyway. So he damned his weakness and damned his sickness and damned the blind shack and the evil old woman inside spying on him.

Better come if you coming.

The golden light had begun to deepen, to redden behind him. Sky dying from fire red to dull grey like a cooling ash. He slouched toward the shack, skirting the remains of the garden, keeping his eyes fixed just ahead of his feet on the smouldering earth. He felt he was being led, felt as he had that night many years before when he stood under the tall trees at the back of his cousins' house, his hand clasped firmly within someone else's, someone who understood his fear, his sudden surges of daring, someone who stood silent and watchful but would not meddle. He believed he was being led, yet he wasn't in tow, wasn't being dragged by the feet.

He passed under the precarious roof of the porch, into its arch of shadow, stepping lightly on the ancient boards which buckled under his feet. The posts supporting the overhang were gaunt as bones, crooked as her cane as they stretched half in crimson light, half in grey shadow from the swaybacked floorboards to the roof. If he huffed and puffed he could blow the whole house down. A pile of old, shrieking wood, a cloud of dust at his feet.

Takes your time, don't you? You moves when you good and ready to move, don't you? You messes in people's wood and sleeps in their sheds like you owns em, don't you, Mister Man? Well you take your time over this bowl of soup. You got from now till dark to finish it and then you're getting on my time. And when you're on my time you got to go.

A shelf is built into the wall beside the thick iron woodstove.
Her soup and her elbow rest on the waist-high slab.

Take my food standing up. You sit down there at the table.
You see that bowl don't you?

Yes, Mam.

Then get to it. Ain't nobody issuing no invitations around
here. And what you see in that bowl is what you get. So go
on and eat.

Yes, Mam.

Takes mine standing up right by the stove. Don't need to
be hauling stuff all round the room and fussing with this and
that to get the table ready. Get my food hot right off the stove
and standing's better for you anyway. Food can go straight
down don't have to be climbing and turning corners and spilling
in the wrong places. Just goes straight down where it's supposed
to go and your belly ain't all twisted like it is sitting in a chair.

He blows on the steaming bowl of soup and blows on the
spoon he dips then raises to his lips. Garlic and pepper and a
rich meat tang float up in the cloud rising off the soup. He had
forgotten the smell of food, forgotten that food could be hot
and rich smelling and full of flavors. The aroma fed him. The
smell of the soup seemed enough.

Don't need to study it. Don't need to talk to it. It's good
soup. It's clean if that's what you looking for.

He wants to say something back to her, but the spoon is too
close to his mouth and his hand is shaking so he leans down
and swallows instead. Everything is in the taste of the soup.
The failing light hovering in the bottom of the rear window
and leaking under the splayed back door, the purple silhouette
of the hills on the horizon, the smoke smell inside the shack,
the hiss of wood in the stove's belly, the old woman's voice
talking to the vegetables she had peeled and sliced and dropped
into bubbling, seasoned stock.

All in the first taste of soup and he wants to tell her that but
he doesn't know how, doesn't know how he can tell her about
all that, about the simple coming together of things unless he
tells her how things can fall apart, but the falling apart is the
story of his trouble and she doesn't want to hear his trouble
so he savors the taste and everything in it a few moments longer
and says:

This sure is good soup, and says, Thank you Mother Bess.

Take your time. Enjoy yourself. Then I want you gone from here.

Light floats in the room, hangs in the darkness like oil twisting in vinegar. The soup burps and the wood hisses in the pit of the stove. Light gathered on her face makes it look greasy. But the light is floating, alive, it draws his eyes away from her lined, old woman's face and plays in the corners, the shadows of the room, focusing on objects, explaining the shape of the space. Light fixes the room's dimensions, uncovers its contents and he thinks of himself as a camera taking the room's picture. But the room won't stay still. He hadn't believed it would be easy. Everybody always said she was mean and half crazy. But he hadn't expected her to be so cold, so far away. He could talk to people. If he had any gift that was it. He could talk to people and they'd like him, they'd talk back and warm up when he smiled. He could get people talking and laughing with him even when they caught him red-handed in something he shouldn't be doing. He could make up something to say that would get a laugh. But Mother Bess just stood there slurping her soup. He mize well be on the moon or some damn place because she paid him no mind, she had shut a door between them and even though he could see through it and hear through it the door was miles thick and strong as iron.

The light that had pointed into the corners of the room, that had glided with a will of its own so his eyes surrendered to it, not knowing why they settled on this patch of crocheted quilt or that silvered edge of bent spoon, the light lost its curiosity, its restlessness and crouched under the dark wings of her hair, her hair parted in the center and framing her forehead like a hood. He knows his skin would sting if she turned her eyes on him. He knows she can feel him staring at her face, greasy and luminous as the light recedes, as the light reddens and deepens and grows too heavy to float. She looks like an old squaw. An old squaw or an old chief because in the movies the only difference is the flowing crown of feathers and that's the only way you can tell whether the old face, cracked and beat up as a mountain, is a man or woman. She has straight hair like an Indian, like all the old people on his mother's side of the family. He has his daddy's hair. Nappy and dirt brown. Combed so it's a cloud over his head, a bushy cloud making him taller than his brothers. He wonders what his hair looks like now.

After the floor of the Bellmawr, the leaves and sawdust of the shed. Like a wild man probably. He can't remember the last time he combed it. The rake was gone, lost somewhere between Indovina's and Bruston Hill. Maybe the cops had it. Maybe Indovina, slick as he is, stabbed the needle-toothed comb into Chubby's heart. He rests the spoon against the inside of the bowl. Both hands dig into the tangled mass, the jungle atop his head.

Sounds like sandpaper. Grit collects beneath his nails, he dislodges a scab. He hunts for bugs scurrying at the roots. Then his face is stinging. She has him lined up over the spoon which she holds to her lips, not drinking, not lowering it but letting it pause against her pursed mouth so she can stare at him like Kilroy peeping over a wall. She is the color of mud now, clay red mud, redder than a comic book Indian, older than anything in Pittsburgh.

If he could think of something to say he'd say it but he can't, even though talk is his gift, so he lowers his hands from his hair, rubs them together beneath the edge of the table and retrieves the spoon from his soup. Which still tastes good. Almost too rich to hold down after so much nothing but still good. He dips in deep for the chunks of vegetables. Watches the freckled skin of the broth break apart like a spider web. Then there is the sound of her, the loud slurping sound of somebody who eats alone. If he made noises like that at the table his mother would yell or slap him if she was close enough. When you're old and alone all the time you get crazy, nasty habits. You get mean and evil. People wouldn't be saying those things all the time if wasn't no truth to it.

If she has a TV or radio or clock he can't find them. Mize well be in the old days when people lived in caves and what not because nothing in the room but a bed and table and chairs look like somebody made out of logs. That's all there is besides the stove and shelves around the walls she mize well be in some wild, old-timey place where niggers still live like Africans or slaves. He looks for a light bulb or a lamp, any sign of electricity, any object which would bring him back to the world, to the time in which he belonged. Could be one of those huts in slave row, one of those niggertown shacks clustered around Massa's big white house. All she needs is a kerchief round her head. All he needs is a watermelon and some chains. If the

city is still there boogeying at the foot of Bruston Hill somebody
has turned the volume down, way down so you can hear the
blood behind your ears and the soup sloshing around in the
emptiness of your belly and the uncouth old woman slurping
her soup spoonful by spoonful without ever blowing on it
though it's hot as fire.

Once upon a time. Once upon a time, he thought, if them
stories I been hearing all my life are true, once upon a time
they said God's green earth was peaceful and quiet. Seems like
people bigger then. They had time to listen, time to talk and
room to move round in. Aunt Aida talking bout people like
they giants. That world was bigger, slower and he'd get jumpy,
get lost in it. Like now in this stillness and quiet each sound
seems too loud, seems strange because the roar of the city isn't
here to drown the noises of his body, the noises of insects and
trees and somebody else's breathing. But once upon a time him
and Sarah alone in the middle of the night. Just the two of them
and the world sleeping and you get mixed up. Can't tell whose
stomach growls, who moans, whose warm juice running down
your thigh. Because it's late and the city's asleep outside the
window, outside the walls. You're in a story. There's room
enough to do what you need to do, what you have to do. Sarah
rolls closer and you can *hear* your fingers stroking her skin,
you can hear the line you trace up her back and over her
shoulder and down her breast. She is big as the sky. You can
hear her nipple stiffening, growing to meet the palm of your
hand. And when you hold your hand lightly above her breast
so it just touches, just barely rubs the hard tip of her softness
you can hear how it feels as your palm circles like coming in
for a landing but no hurry, no rush, just gliding in slow circles
in the air while you listen.

The stillness unbroken. Sarah rolls closer to him and rises
slightly on her elbow so the ring of darker brown around her
nipples is visible an instant as the covers fall away from her
brown shoulders and he swallows hard because those soft eyes
on her chest have a way of seeing through him and around him
and taking his breath away. No matter how many times he
stares at them or fondles them or mashes them with his chest
when he's inside her. He swallows hard in the stillness because
he is seeing another life, a life long gone. Then he is nothing.
Smaller than nothing and alone. Stories are lies and Mother

Bess pigging down her soup brings him back. Her loud slurping on the soup drowns the noise of his blood, the noise of his heart.

You make some dynamite soup, Mother Bess. It's not him talking. It's some jive, jack-leg preacher grinning and wiping grease from his liver lips and rolling his eyeballs at the platter of fried chicken he's already eaten half of. Yes, Mam, and I surely wouldn't mind helping myself to another piece. Rolling his eyes and showing his teeth and wiping his greasy chin on his handkerchief. Yes, Mam. Umm Ummm Mammy Bess. And he listens to the voice and it's not his but he can't remember what his should sound like so the voice keeps talking and he is ashamed, but talk is his gift, if he has a gift, so the voice continues its shuffling, its buck and wing, its step and fetchit grinning.

Till she cuts him off. Till she speaks from her post beside the stove, her elbow still leaning on the shelf where her empty bowl rests.

When you finish you bring that bowl up here. That's all there is and ain't nothing else. Just set it here by mine. We ain't got no waitress service here. I don't like to cook. Never did and never will. Don't like people talking about my cooking, neither. If people like what I fix they can eat. If they don't they can leave it setting. Don't like all that Mother Bess stuff neither. Wish I knew who started that Mother Bess mess. I ain't nobody's mama. Was once but that was a million pitiful years ago and ain't nobody on this earth got the right going around calling me mother now. I told them that. Don't know how many times I told them. But it's Mother Bess this and Mother Bess that like I ain't got sense enough to know my own name and they ain't got sense to listen when I tell them I ain't nobody's mama.

Hey, didn't mean no harm. Just trying to be sociable. You know, didn't mean to call you out your name. Like that's what I been hearing since I was a little kid. Mother Bess. All I ever heard.

Well, you heard wrong.

Sorry then. Didn't know you had a thing about your name.

Ain't had a name since those fools down there started with that Mother Bess stuff.

What you want me to call you then?

Don't need be calling me nothing cause I want you gone

from here in a few short minutes. Be dark in a few minutes. Already getting dark in here.

Turn on some light, then.

Don't need lights. When it's dark people supposed to sleep.

Bet you ain't got no electricity.

They run a wire up here and it's still here far as I know but I sleeps when it's night the way decent people supposed to. Don't like no lectricity.

Sure a lot of things you don't like.

I suppose that's my business.

Tell me something you do like. Tell me something good before you run me away from here. I ain't heard nothing good for days. Tell me something you like.

What I like is what I got. I like peace and quiet and being left alone.

Must get lonely up here all by yourself.

And I like minding my own business. And other people minding theirs.

Hey, I'm just trying to be sociable.

You got a busy mouth.

Yeah. That's what I got alright. A busy mouth and a world of trouble. You got that right. But ain't nothing wrong with needing to talk. Told you I'm in real trouble. If you had a TV or a radio up here, you'd know. You probably the only one in Pittsburgh don't know by now. There's a man dead down there and the police after me because they think I did it. I'm running for my life and I'm scared.

I think running make more sense than talking.

I am running, I'm running so hard I feel like I'm coming apart. Everything I got's running. Hands, heart, eyeballs. Everything you see and don't see is running so hard I can't think straight. You see a man sitting at this table but that sitting man is moving faster than you ever seen anybody move. But ain't no place to run. Running fast as I can but I'm standing still cause ain't no place to run.

I see you sitting there. And I know who you are. Just exactly who you are.

Tell me about it.

You Lizabeth's son, Thomas. Your grandmother was my sister's girl. You wasn't even close to born when my sister Gert died. Freeda was her oldest. And some say the prettiest in her quiet way. John French your granddaddy. Strutting around in that big brown hat like he owned Homewood. Hmmph. Tell me I don't know. Know you coming and going. You a Lawson now. You and your three brothers and your sister in the middle. Don't know if she's Lawson now or not. Girls these days always marrying, always changing names like it makes a difference. Don't know what name she goes by but I know her too. I was there when your mama Lizabeth first seen the light of day. Snow was seven feet deep. You couldn't see people walking in the ditches they plowed. Snowing so hard and the wind blowing like to tore down that shack on Cassina Way. Lizabeth was Freeda's first. Came out blue as that shirt you're wearing. Yes indeed. Know all about it. I was there when that simpleminded May grabbed her up and run out in the snow. She did it so fast nobody raised a hand to stop her. Just grabbed up that tiny little sky blue baby and runned out the front door before anybody got their mouth open to say stop. Stuck that poor little naked thing down in a pile of snow and don't you know that blue child started to breathe. She started to breathe outside in all that snow and cold and freezing wind and been breathing ever since. That's your mama. And I know just who you are too.

I heard that story before. Heard Aunt Aida tell something like that. Didn't believe it. She's always talking some off the wall, old time mess like that.

Well, I ain't just talking. I'm a witness and couldn't care less what you believe. Your believes is your business. But I say what I know, not what I heard.

Sure ain't gon sit here and argue with you. If you was there you was there. All that old time stuff don't make me no nevermind. Wasn't even born yet.

You wasn't thought of. I'm talking about your mama. About the first time your mama seen the light of day and screamed to tell the world she was here.

Put her in the snow.

That's right. Stuck her in a snowdrift like you'd duck a doughnut in your coffee.

Damn. In a pile of snow.

With the wind howling and beating on the boards of that shack on Cassina. Like to blowed it down. Front door just about tore off its hinges when May run through and had your mama dipped down in that snow before anybody could holler,

Stop fool. Wasn't for that crazy May wouldn't be no Lizabeth and you wouldn't be sitting here neither.

Wouldn't be running neither.

Now don't put that on May nor your mama nor nobody else. You the one done whatever devilment you done. You the one got to pay now.

Need me a few days. Few days to catch up on sleep and get my head together. Won't be asking nothing else from you. I know how take care myself. Just need a few days.

Dark in here. And dark is my bedtime.

You a hard woman.

Life's hard. Didn't nobody never tell you? Didn't nobody never hold you up and look in your eyes and tell you you got to die one day little boy and they be plenty days you wish it be sooner stead of later? Didn't nobody never tell you that? Feel sorry for you if you a grown man and nobody ain't told you that.

Been told lots of things. But nobody got to tell me it's hard. Out here in the streets my whole life. I know it's mean out here.

You still a baby.

Well there's cops out there looking to kill this baby. And nobody ain't gon save me by sticking my ass in no snow pile. Old people always talking like they the only ones ever know trouble. Talking like the only hurt is the hurt put on them. Been hearing that jive all my life. About suffering and waiting. Like I ain't been suffering and waiting myself. Like I got all the time in the world. Like I got to suffer a little more and wait a little longer and...and what...what's supposed to happen after I suffer some more and wait some more? Tired of that bullshit.

Watch your mouth. You ain't in no barn.

I'm tired. Tired of it.

I'm tired too. And you crowding my bedtime.

You do all that talking about knowing who I am. You tell those stories and you still gon put me out in the street. You a hard woman. Don't understand you.

Hard and evil and crazy. Just like they say.

Well shit. I ain't begging.

This ain't no barn.

You got a glass for some water? If you can spare the water.

Rinse the bowl. Ain't no waitress service.

Damn.

Get your water. And don't be wasting your breath damning nothing in my house. Git your water and git.

He stands at the sink which gurgles like somebody has the pipe in a stranglehold, then as if the death grip is suddenly released, the spigot spatters him, the gagged, pent-up water splashes his pants and wets his arm and then trickles into the bowl, a trickle he mops around to rinse its insides. The water is nasty. He chugalugs, trying not to taste it but he can smell it and his mouth is full of old pennies. He spits into the sink and wants to wash out his mouth but there is only the nasty water dribbling from the faucet.

Her back is towards him. She is broad and short, squat like a beetle reared up on its hind legs. Her back hard as a beetle's back in the darkness across the room. He has the urge to stride across the room and hit her once, slam his fist into the dark shell. The blow would clang, like hitting one of those old-timey knights in their iron suits. Just once to let her know what he could do if he wanted to. The world was hard, sure nuff. He knew all about that. Harder even than the shell wrapped around her old, thick back. World could bust her up. His fist could smash her dark shell into a thousand pieces. If not his fist then something harder, like the long handled steam iron the light had picked out on one of the shelves. It would be easy to knock her down. Nobody would miss her. She lived up here all alone. Evil and crazy. Could take what she wouldn't give. World was that hard. This Mother Bess who didn't want to be called Mother Bess, who was she anyway? What was she to him? Except somebody in his way. Somebody mean and crazy whose stubborn ways were pushing him towards his enemies.

That's how hard the world was. He could knock down this old bitch and take what she wouldn't give. Just cause she was there when his mother was born, just cause she told crazy stories and knew his name and the names of his brothers and sisters. What did any of that mean? What did it weigh? There were people out to kill him and some Mother Bess who was nobody's mama, who was nothing, who was old enough to be dead, who was she to stand in his way?

He coughed. The gritty water was stuck in his throat. In the silence, the stillness, he thought the cough would startle her, as it startled him. Make her turn around and face him and see how close he was to splitting that old beetle back, how easy it would be. But nothing moved. As crazy as she was she just might sleep standing up like a horse. All night the dark mass of her hulking beside the bed like a ghost haunting somebody asleep under the covers. Instead of a clang, instead of the brittle armor of an insect, his fist would pass through her. It would be like pounding at a door which suddenly opens. And the force of his blow, the lunge of his body into the punch would pull him into empty space, through her and falling forever.

He trips again over the rags beside the back door, slams the door behind him, and sinks again into the swaying boards before he stumbles off the lip of porch into the night.

CLEMENT

▼▼▼

Clement is counting like that Count Dracula puppet they got on Sesame Street who's always counting everything. This time it's the balls of black wool he sweeps from the floor of Big Bob's barbershop. He is counting them as he stuffs them into a gigantic pillowcase. When he's done the pillow will be big enough to sleep on. A soft, cushioning bed in the back of Big Bob's and he'll throw away the skinny mattress spotted with bed bug blood and his blood. The balls are fuzzy soft and clean. Not like the wire and Brillo shit he usually brooms from the mottled green tiles. By late afternoon the balls of hair are dusty, matted with filth, but these are perfect. They even smell good. Not the smell of pomade and hair tonic and grease but popcorn, popcorn fresh from the glass tank at the movies. His bed will be white and soft. Like Violet's titties when she leans on the bar and squeezes her blouse between her arms so they sit there like a pillow. Clement feels himself sinking. Into the softness. Into the velvet blackness which lives inside the mirror. Lives inside her white blouse. A million Clements like the million shiny glasses stacked on the counter behind the bar and each one asleep, each one peaceful and dreaming like the glasses inside the mirror.

BESS

▼▼▼

She does not dress or undress. Her man's eyes are not watching from the bed. He's not lying there with his hands ready to run up under her flannel gown, ready to undress her again when she's warm under the covers, so she doesn't undress because she never dresses she just puts something on and one day she remembers to take it off again. At night it's the buttons of a housecoat undone one by one by her clumsy fingers. She can get lost between buttons. A thought will come to her and fill her and when it leaves and she remembers again to unfasten the next button it will seem like years since she's undone the one before. Some of the rags missing half their buttons. Sometimes she's mad she'll just rip one open, split the front and shrug it off her shoulders and it'll be lying there in the morning like a skin she's shed and good for nothing no more. Sometimes her fingers so swoll up and ain't been warm all day she'll pull a flannel gown over top of what she's got on and sleep like that and pretend she doesn't care. She would have offered the pitiful thing some whiskey. She almost did when he asked for water and almost did again when she heard the faucet burst on and heard him drinking like water was going out of style. Some of Henry Bow's moonshine fix him up good. Burn his nasty mouth. Chase them scared rabbits out his eyes. But then he'd be sitting again and staying longer and if you offer one drink you probably got to offer him another. Next thing you know he's pouring his own and you got company for the night so she had just listened to him finish and set down the bowl and slam the door like some ungrateful pup. And that was that and now she got these buttons to fool with and Clement in the morning and that dry space before she dies into sleep, that space all the whiskey Henry Bow got won't fill.

TOMMY

▼▼

He knew it was up there. That giant swollen frog of a water tower perched on its stilt legs. In the moonlight it looked even more like a frog. A frog somebody had made out of stuff from a junkyard. A giant soldered together frog made by somebody afraid of frogs. He knew it was up there but hadn't seen it all day till just this moment when its long shadow stretched down the hillside and he looked up from the black reflection into the sky which harbored its black silhouette. He had heard stories about kids climbing the tower. Long time ago when there was still a big house and still lots of his people on top of Bruston Hill. It could look like a frog or look like a teapot. A skinny ladder twisted up one side. Have to be crazy to go up that thing. The first time he'd seen it he'd asked what it was but nobody could tell him exactly or tell him how they filled it or why it was there growing in the middle of trees and bushes. Like a spaceship or some damn thing crash-landed and got stranded up there in the middle of those crazy people lived like hermits up on Bruston Hill. The water tower was grey and rusty. Nobody could tell him how much it held, or why it was there. Even now, even grown he hesitated at the edge of its shadow. A black shape which would soon be swallowed in the deeper blackness falling on Bruston Hill. That's all it was, etched there momentarily in the failing light. But he retreated, he stared and then backed off. If anything could have started him up that curling ladder it would be those questions he asked a long time ago. Nobody had answered them then. Nobody since. You'd have to get up there and see for yourself. You'd have to get up high enough to lift the lid and peek over the edge. The tower was the only thing taller than the trees at the back of her yard, the trees he used for guiding his steps back where he'd come from.

II

BESS

▼▼▼▼▼▼▼▼▼▼▼▼▼▼▼▼▼▼▼▼▼▼▼▼▼▼▼▼▼▼▼▼▼▼▼▼▼▼

Don't you think I knew you was out there? Don't you think I saw those long feet sticking out my shed? How you gon hide those long feet, those long legs? I knew you was out there. Where else you gon be?

She said it to herself a dozen times before she said it to him. And didn't say it to him when she shook him awake. No, she was quiet then, quiet as the morning which wasn't even morning yet, quiet as dawn, as the dew and darkness still hanging on when she wrapped her sweater around the nightgown and pulled on her coat over both and shuffled outside in her slippers to shake him awake. She was as quiet as the half sleep world when she took hold to the stick leaning against her bed and dragged it and dragged herself out to the shed where she knew he'd be sleeping. That quiet when she grabbed his shoulders like she grabbed the stick laid beside her bed in case him or some other nigger was crazy enough to try and take her house, grabbed the knob of bone in his shoulder which felt like the knob of her walking stick and shook him awake without saying what she'd said a dozen times to herself beginning when she dreamed the feet and again when she looked through the walls, through the black night and saw them poking out her shed and again when she made herself awake, made herself struggle with the sweater and pull on the coat saying it a dozen times at least before she crossed to the shed and shook him awake. And didn't say it out loud till he was sitting at the table again like something the cat drug in and she was starting a fire in the stove because he sat there shivering, his eyes closed, a shadow hardly more real than the shapes moving on the ceiling as the stove flared to life and she got the kettle and got that water going.

91

Then she spoke to the shadow as if speaking to it might stop
its shivering, make it real.

Don't you think I knew you was out there? Don't you think
I saw those long feet sticking out my shed? How you gon hide
those long feet, those long legs? I knew you was out there.
Where else you gon be?

His eyes are sleep-dulled. His flesh is puffy like it'd come
off in dirty hunks if you pulled it. Pimply where the beard
starts on his cheeks. She has good eyes but she lights the lamp
for him and the yellow light claws one side of his face, stripping
the skin, baring the scars, the pimples, the craters, the splinters
of hair growing every which way.

What'd you do that for old woman? Why'd you wake me
up and bring me in here for? I was dreaming. I was having a
good dream and now you got me up and got me in here so you
can tell me Git out again.

Hush, you. I knowed all along you was out there and knowed
you ain't got the blood for it. Blood's too thin for sleeping
outdoors. Look at you shaking like a leaf. Ain't no warmth in
the ground yet. Ground's warm in the day after the sun been
on it awhile but ain't no warmth seeped down deep yet. That
ice still close under there. You can't see it but you can feel it
at night. Look at you.

If you know so much why'd you put me out in the first
place?

Just hush.

Ain't much better in here. Like a damned icebox in here.

Pull you off one of them blankets off the bed. You got that
thin blood. That's the problem.

Problem is you sent me out in the cold in the first place.

Stove gon heat up the place real quick.

Shit. Tell that to my teeth. Maybe they stop clicking. Maybe
I won't freeze to death before it gets hot in here.

You sitting there like some Indin chief wrapped up in *my*
blanket, at *my* table in *my* house and I got *my* weary old bones
scampering around starting up *my* stove and fixing *my* coffee
so's you can get something warm in *your* belly and you got
the nerve to be signifying like the ungrateful pup you are.

What kind of game you playing, old woman? First you kick
my butt out in the cold. Kick me out and tell me I was born
to die and all that mess now you tell me you fixing me coffee

and fussing over my thin blood. Don't know where you coming
from. What kind of a game you playing?

Course I knew you was out there. Had to be there if there
wasn't no place else to go. So just hush now and don't worry
me while I'm fixing this coffee.

She lifts the cloth tacked like a curtain between two corner
shelves and extracts a big jar of instant coffee and one of Henry
Bow's jugs. The soup bowls are coffee mugs now and she
sticks a spoon in each.

You got to cut this nasty water. Ain't nothing in it to hurt
you. Minerals in it probably good for you, they taste so bad.
Can't drink it less I cut it.

So it's whiskey first gurgling from the jug. Then she pours
from the kettle and then the coffee is last, sprinkled straight
from the jar. The spoons are for stirring and for tasting which
she does without even blowing on the brew steaming in the
spoon.

I can still taste it.

And it's whiskey again, a good splash for her, a gurgle
more for him and it's done.

Hey you. Don't be falling to sleep at my table. You so
pitiful this morning. Here. Take this coffee. This'll thicken up
your blood if you got any blood to thicken.

Then you gon let me stay here awhile?

You got my blanket wrapped around you. You sitting at my
table drinking my coffee. I guess you might say you done
moved in real comfortable.

I need to stay a few days. A few days till I get my head
together.

You mean till hell freezes over. You mean till I'm dead and
in my grave. Don't know nothing about that getting your head
together mess. Head could use a combing if that's what you
mean.

You know what I'm talking about.

Yes I do. Course I do. Know more about it than you. Lived
too long and seen too much to believe a couple days on top
of this hill gon change anything.

All I need's a little time. Little peace so I can stop running.

Listen at you. Listen at this poor child. The day you die is
the day you stop running. And not one second sooner. You
mize well go on back to that shed and start to dreaming again.

You said it was a good dream didn't you. Cause that's as close as you gon get to standing still in this life. Mize well go on back there and start dreaming again.

You call this coffee, old woman?

Don't call it nothing. I drinks it. And if you don't like it don't say nothing, don't give it no name, just set it down.

I ain't complaining. Just saying it's strong, is all. And strong ain't hardly the word. This coffee got four feet and all of em kicking.

Water ain't good less you cut it. Coffee taste like rusty nails you don't cut it.

Well, you sure did slice this up right. You done carved it up in silver bullets and they gon make me happy if they don't kill me first.

Like two days on this hill gon make a difference. Like running ain't what every soul on God's green earth set here to do all the days of his life. Mize well go back to dreaming.

Leave my dreams alone, now. Don't need nobody getting in my dreams.

I know all bout you.

Well you sure in hell don't know nothing bout my dreams. Unless you a witch or some damn thing.

Watch your mouth.

Then leave my dreams alone. Don't be telling me you know what nobody in the world knows but me. How you know what's in my head? Got a son down there you don't know nothing about. Clyde. Be five in February. Aquarius, the water sign. His mama into astrology. She used to read all the books. Spooky how that stuff come true sometimes. She the one into it but she be talking all the time. Aquarius and it's funny cause I was dreaming bout the ocean and the beach and Clyde with me. Wasn't no beach like Chicken Bone in Atlantic City where niggers laid out side by side like they so used to the ghetto they get to all that open space they got to crowd up under one another to feel at home. Nothing like that. This was like those tropical paradises you see in magazines and what not. Like they got in ads telling you to fly here and fly there and you ain't even got bus fare in your pocket. A beach like that. All golden sand and palm trees and not a soul in sight. Not even that fine chick in a bikini they got in all the ads. Golden beach and blue waves and blue sky and just me and Clyde walking in wet sand with our shoes off and shirts off. He be smiling

up at me and be listening to myself telling a story. You know
how you in two places at once in a dream. Like that. Yeah.
Me telling him a story and me listening too. Like really three
people there and one like God or somebody so he can be on
the beach and somewhere else too. Telling a story make Clyde
happy. No fairy tale or nonsense like that. Telling him bout
life. Real life. When life was good. When life full of good
things and safe. And the story ain't just words. More like it
is in them old songs. What made the story so good was that
other me listening too. Watching over me and my son. The
other me like some kind of god floating in the air so I could
listen and make everything true. So I could make it happen.

Don't want to hear your troubles.

That ain't trouble. That's what I was dreaming till you come
pulling on my foot. And you don't know nothing about it.

That's your trouble too. You just don't know it. You just
don't understand yet what trouble is. That dreaming. That
dreaming's where trouble start.

Already told you they after me. Them trigger-happy cops
is what I call trouble.

You one comes and goes as you pleases, ain't you? Saw
that from the first. Been knowing that since I first laid eyes on
you. Come and go in your own good time.

I ain't begging no more. And I wish to hell I did have
someplace else to go besides this godforsaken hilltop and that
freezing barn like some slave or some wild animal sleeping
outside.

Look you. Don't be telling me about your rather this and
your rather that and your dreaming and where you'd rather be
if you had all your rathers. I came up on this hill to die. Brought
everything I needed with me. And this place up here is a
graveyard full up with rathers. Brought everything I need. Not
everything I want. Didn't say that. Said everything I need.
What I want is buried in the cold ground. That's where my
rathers is and that's where they gon stay till I get down there
with them. Then I have all my rathers. So don't be telling me
what you *would* if you *could*. Knew you was out there in the
shed. Where else you gon be? Ain't no other way it could be.
So here you is and here I is and that's that. So hush about
rathers and drink your coffee.

CLEMENT

▼▼

In the Brass Rail Clement hears the train less than a block away rattling across the tracks over Homewood Avenue, hears it coming behind a whistle and diesel shriek. No music, no traffic outside on Homewood Avenue. Noise of the train snatches the walls off the Brass Rail and you believe this the way the world ends, this how Big Foot Death come after you and jerk you away. After the train passes there are wavy lines and dots and buzzing like when the TV fucks up. So he waits for everything to get fixed. Waits for Carl's finger to start playing in the mouth of his Iron City bottle again, waits for Carl to finish what he was saying to his feet, waits for big-tittied Violet, doubled in the mirror, the front of her real, the back of her glowing in the dark glass, he waits for her to finish wiping the shot glass she has in her hand, wipe it and set it with the others she been polishing, set it with the million others in the mirror holding her white back. Clement's holding his breath too and might die unless somebody put a key in the lock and turn it so he can go on about his business. But things start up again. Carl mutters to his foot again and Clement sees the hand of the wall clock fall from one minute to the next so it's three minutes after eleven. It's almost afternoon and soon he better be climbing up that hill. Soon Miss Bess be calling cause she said tomorrow afternoon.

May day getting hot as June and Violet say she can't turn on the fan cause L.T. said Don't care if niggers be melting into puddles of grease. L.T. own the Brass Rail and he didn't care how hot it got the air conditioning wasn't coming on till the day it always came on and that won't be for two more weeks she said. Shoot, she said, if it was up to me I'd have it on. I'm here all day and I'd have it on. She said I don't know if it's better to have the door open or shut. It's shut now keeping out

96

the white morning light. Carl still talking to his feet but loud enough for Clement or anybody else to listen if they want to. Then to Violet. Babe, bring me over another one of them Rocks. It was the third Rolling Rock nip to go with the double McNaughton's he ordered when Clement came in at three minutes to ten. Counting was one thing to do in the Brass Rail. Easy to keep up when just a few people like now. But Violet had sent Clement to Footer's with her pants suit. Footer's was where they footerized your clothes which meant you could get them back that same night clean as new. She sent him so he couldn't say for sure. Might be three Rocks. Might be four and maybe Carl had another double McNaughton's cause don't take him but a second to chugalug the double shot glass. Carl let it sit there for a long time, not touching it or looking at it. Like maybe he don't like it, or forgot it, or maybe Violet put the whiskey down front the wrong person. He let it sit there long as a hour sometimes then he snatch it up and drain it in a breath and she pour him another so he can pay it no mind. Clement keeps score and listens. Violet let him have a Seven-up from out the case in the back. Peedy warm but sweet. Got his thumb down in the bottle now. Like to make the poop sound. Like to make the sound of the train whistle coming through a tunnel with his top lip over the bottle mouth and blowing down in it.

Hey, Carl, you hear anything about Chester?

They got that Negro under the jail, babe. Bondsman won't touch him. Not even that bloodsucker Alphonse.

Why'd Chester go and do something like that?

All of us out here a little crazy but you got to be more than a little crazy to shoot your partner and call the police and tell them to come and get you.

Ain't the way I heard it. According to what I heard the cops made a mistake. Raided the wrong place and busted in shooting and killed Dupree and half-killed Chester and now they trying to blame it on Chester.

Well Dupree's dead and who's gon believe Chester? You got the cops story and that's the way it will go down.

Clement had seen the spinning red lights two days before, the black and whites parked back to back and on the sidewalks and catty-corner blocking streets and alleys. He'd heard the guns popping like firecrackers and the sirens and the big voice in a bull-horn like on TV. In the doorway of the apartment building on Bennett and Kelley, stuffed in a doorway on the stone steps with a bunch of people because it was close enough to see the blood and you could stick your head out of the doorway till the cops shooed you back. Standing next to a funky old man got wine all down his T-shirt. Guns popping and the old dude grabbing at this purple belly and giggling. They got me, ooh, they got me.

Yeah, babe. It's summertime sure enough. When colored folks start to killing each other two a day you know summertime's here. Too cold for all that mess till summertime. Ain't no robins come to Homewood for years but you know when summer comes. Niggers start dying like flies. Two a day.

Nobody heard from your Tommy yet?

Not yet, Lord help him. He still out there in the street. Those dirty dogs still hunting him down and I know Tommy ain't killed nobody.

It's a shame.

Worse than that. Worse than the worse you could imagine, girl. It's a damn crying shame. Ain't been over to my sister's yet today. Know I should go over there but she's just coming apart. She was pitiful last night. We all sat up with her after the police left. My heart ain't hard enough today. Can't watch what this mess doing to her.

Always falls hardest on the mama. On the family.

Well, Tommy ain't too happy neither. Wherever he is. Don't know what I want. If they catch him they gon put him under the jail. No little wrist slap nine months like he got last time. But if they don't catch him and put him away he's just a walking target. One them pigs shoot Tommy down and get a medal and nobody gon ask no questions. Just a matter of time.

The ghost he heard yesterday morning has a name. Same name they talking bout in Big Bob's. Clement doesn't tell Carl that Tommy is dead already, a ghost already up on Bruston Hill in Miss Bess's house. Ain't nobody's business. Because when you do train noise deep in the bottle you could make the train fall from the sky and land on the bridge over Homewood Avenue like it does dropping like a cat with all four feet spinning before it hits the ground.

Clement watches Carl watch a man come in the door. Tall man in a suit ducked in the door and looked around real careful like maybe he in the wrong place, like maybe he subject to turn around and split somebody yell *Boo* real loud. But he lets the door swing shut behind him and tips in and sits beside Carl.

Violet. This my nephew, John. This Tommy's brother from out of town.

And the tall dude how-do-you-dos and pleased-to-meet-you or some such off the wall do like that and Violet plays it back perfect like she been saying such stuff all her life.

Man don't even order a drink. He just gets in Carl's ear and Carl twisting his big butt this way and that like the stool getting hot up under his buns.

Then Carl start to working his knees. Big thighs flapping like butterfly wings. Getting faster and faster like they pumping something to his mouth. Like he got to be working real hard down there under the bar so his mouth can make that lazy kind of Carl talk. You ain't never sure another word coming. They take they own good time. Don't know if Carl finished talking or just resting he take so long between words. And the man mize well stop whispering cause Carl tells everybody everything anyway. Tell his feet if nobody else listen. That loud slow Carl talk you be hearing even if you ain't listening. You be in the back peeing you still hear Carl preaching and that tall dude draws back like he don't know nobody talk that loud.

Your mama told you right. This just where I be most the time. Got my little throne here. You know what I mean?

Tall dude act like he ain't with Carl now. Sitting up straight-backed. Peeling at that label. *Budweiser, please* is what he ordered. And Violet bringing him a beer and a glass just as nice. He don't say Rock or Bud or Iron like somebody got good sense. He have to go and say *Budweiser, please* like Violet supposed to set something different on the bar nobody else ain't drinking.

Clement sees the Tommy face behind Miss Bess's wall now. The Tommy they all talking about. Miss Bess said come tomorrow afternoon and the ghost be gone.

Oh yeah. Yeah. Yeah. You know something, babe. I'm getting absentminded and pickle-brained as them old folks used to crack me up. Guess I'm one now. Old like Aunt Aida and the rest. You know how Aunt Aida was. And there was her sister Aunt Gert. She was your great-grandmother, but you wouldn't remember Aunt Gert, bless her soul. Aida and Bess and Gert and Gaybrella. All them Hollinger sisters a little nutty. Never knew what they'd say next. You got that science fiction mess these days but let me tell you Aunt Aida the original time traveler. She was a sure nuff trip. Aida be standing there looking you in the face having a conversation with somebody been dead thirty years. She always loved Tommy special. Bet she was wild like him in her day. Always asking after Tommy that first time he was in the slammer. She got so much in her head, can't keep it straight. It's funny too. Tommy used to visit Aunt Aida regular. No time for nobody else in the family but he'd take that baby of his over there see Aunt Aida. Never could understand that one. Running wild but always found time to see Aunt Aida. Half the time the poor old thing wouldna knowed whether the devil or Abraham Lincoln be knocking at her door.

The man beside Carl is listening with his head down. Stripping the label from his bottle of beer. His is Budweiser. *Budweiser, please.*

Violet babe, why don't you get up off some of those quarters?

L.T. don't like me using bar change in the jukebox till there's plenty customers.

You know I'm the best customer L.T. got. And my nephew here lives out with the white folks in Colorado. He don't get much soul music where he's at. He's the only colored out there and I know they don't allow no nigger music on the radio.

Colorado.

Yeah. Out west with the rich white folks.

You like it out there?

Course he does. No garbage in the streets, no junkies going through your mailbox. Wish I lived someplace they run all the trifling niggers away at sundown.

Violet says Hush Carl and tells the man she's sorry his brother in trouble. She whispers. Everything is whisper after Carl's big mouth. She don't smile, don't flirt at the stranger. When Violet smiles you see gaps and a broken tooth. But she don't care. She's good at flirting. Nobody counts her teeth. Don't like her smile she'll say *kiss my ass* in a minute. She's serious now. No flirt. No smile. When she leans over the bar like she's doing now looks like a pillow sitting there. White blouse with purple flowers. Titties like a pillow when she leans with her elbows on the bar and listens up close in the man's face.

Thank you. I appreciate your concern. And it's Wyoming, not Colorado.

Bet it's nice out there. Bet it's clean.

It's a good place to raise children.

Ain't that nice.

Her elbows are on the bar and her titties squeezed between them, glowing like her back glows in the dark mirror. She smiles now and wants to hear more. She is batting her eyelashes and as close to the man as the bar she keeps polished and shining will let her get. He sit straight on his stool. He don't lean away but he don't get down neither. If a train came now and hooted loud like they do, bet he'd jump ten feet in the air cause he can't get closer and he better not lean back so there ain't no room for him. Stool mize well be a pin head.

He's a nice man, Carl. Then her eyes in the mirror, winking at Carl. Carl's eyes in there following her. In the dark mirror with those shiny rows of glasses and the soft white pillow.

Mind's getting limpy as my feet. How many times you told me Wyoming? Know damned well youall live in Wyoming. You been out there what . . . two, three years now. Moved out West when Tommy had his first trouble. Yeah. And I still go and say Colorado. You know what it is, babe? All them places sound alike. That's what it is. I think Wild West and white folks, and one place sound just as good as the other.

Three years.

Brain getting bad as my feet. Got shots for a while but they still swell up soon as it's hot. Feet ain't worth a damn. It's all I can do to get myself to work. Old man Strayhorn told me once the worse kind of pain was foot pain cause a poor man always got to use his feet. Seems like since my feet been bad I got to do more walking than I ever did in my life. Walk to work. Walk to the clinic for my methadone. Be sitting at home wanting a Rock so bad I can taste it. But I just sit there thinking and smacking my lips a half hour before these feet decide to walk cross the floor.

Terrible how they do you. They just stick you in jail and let you rot. Wasn't nothing wrong with my feet till I went to jail. Went through the war and everything. In the jungle and the ocean and done every kind of nasty work a poor man has to do to stay alive. Went through all that and my feet fine till they rotted in the goddamn jail. Jail's a killer. Jail eats you up. Hope Tommy's a thousand miles away. Hope he's halfway to Timbuktu and ain't looking back.

I guess it's good that Tommy knows his way around. That should help.

Oh yeah. Your brother ain't no baby. He been in the joint before. He know his way around, alright. Trouble is he know too much. Know what it's like behind them bars.

But he'd be safer there than where he is right now. Wherever that is. While he's running he's in danger of getting gunned down by a cop.

Hope he's a thousand miles away from here.

They don't always ask questions first.

You got that right. These Wyatt Earp Marshall Dillon motherfuckers don't like nothing better than blowing away a nigger if he look at them cross-eyed. We got plenty niggers dead resisting arrest. Hope that boy's long gone from here.

Then you don't know anything? Haven't heard anything?

Wish I knew. Wish I got a post card from Hawaii or some damn place ten thousand miles away.

Mom worries that they'll bring him home dead. She says she can't sleep because every time she closes her eyes she sees him in a box, dead in a box.

Your mama always was the worrying kind. Your mama always did feel things more than other folks. She bleeds for people. My big sister's a worrier like her mama and always will be and ain't nothing nobody can do about that. Is her blood pressure up?

Sky high.

Well you make sure she stay on her medicine. Make sure she don't stop. When she gets real down she tell herself medicine don't do no good. She stop taking it you don't stay on her. That boy's gon feel worse than he do now if something happen to his mama.

Sometimes I get close to hating him. Everything inside me gets cold and I don't care what happens to him. I think about all he's done, all the people he's hurt. The way Mom is now. And that man who got killed in the robbery. I know it's not all Tommy's fault. I know he's a victim in a way too. But on the other hand he's hurt people and done wrong and he can't expect to just walk away. But he does think he can walk away. Like he walked away from his wife and son. He's still like a child. He always wanted every day to be a party. A party from morning till night. He'd wake up looking for the party. It's that attitude I hate, not him. I want Tommy to live, to have a chance. I want him to be a thousand miles away too, but I want him to see what he's done. I want him to take responsibility.

Wish I knew something to tell you. Wish I could say something to make it better.

I ought to go soon. I'll be staying at my mother's for the next few days. Or until something breaks.

Well I'ma come over later and sit with Lizabeth. She'll listen to me sometimes.

Quarters clink in the jukebox. They are heavy and don't fall straight. Whole machine shakes when a quarter falls, you can hear it hit the dead ends and bang over the edges like somebody made out of metal tripping down steps. Colored lights dance across the top of the jukebox and do funny things to Violet's face. She studying the numbers and letters you push to get your record. Her shoulders shake when the music come on. She's shivering beside the jukebox like somebody just opened the front door and let the Hawk fly in. She wrap her arms around herself and squeeze her own titties. Then the Hawk gone and she ain't shaking she's smiling that big-mouthed, gappy Violet smile and playing the row of buttons like they was a piano. Long green nails tapping the buttons and the wheels inside the jukebox turning and spinning out colored lights in her face.

Play B–12, babe.

This ain't no Bingo Game.

Go on, play it. You know that's my tune, babe. Push it three or four times and bring your fine self back here and lay one of those Rocks on me. (Four?)

Colored people is a shame. Minute ago you begging me to play the jukebox for you and your nice nephew. No sooner I start to doing that you crying for me behind the bar.

B–12, sweets.

You know I played it, man. You know I ain't hardly not played it with you sitting here. Wonder B–12 ain't wore out.

Good ones don't never wear out. Good ones might stretch a little but you sure can't wear them out.

Go on with your nasty self, Carl.

Ain't nothing nasty about it. The truth ain't never nasty. It just be the truth.

Listen to him. Listen to this man trying to sound heavy. You trying to show off for your nephew. He's an educated man. I can tell that just by looking at him. Now I bet he could get real heavy if he wanted to. Shy as he is I bet he could talk that talk if he wanted to.

Violet is behind the bar again. Talking loud to somebody else down the other end. Music makes it harder to hear what people saying so Clement just leans back in the booth, runs his tongue down in the Seven-up for that last bit of sugar if his thumb ain't pooped it all out. Carl pours the Rolling Rock into his glass. (Four?) He tilts his glass so it won't be all foam. The color is pee. Beer going in and beer coming out look the same. That's why he don't drink it. He just takes a glass of sweet wine when he can get it. If wine come back out you'd be dead because wine coming out would be blood.

Ain't sweet at all so he pulls back his tongue and pokes out his lip and the train starts through the tunnel. Slow and soft at first but then he blows harder and it's haul-assing. Shake the Brass Rail just like a real train.

What you doing, Clement? Don't you be making that noise when B–12 comes on. Didn't even know that boy was still behind me till he start to making all that noise. Young boy like him oughtn't be hanging around in no bar all day.

Where he supposed to be then? Out on the corner shooting dope like the rest of these hoodlums his age. Clement's alright just where he is.

Hey Clement. Stop that foolishness and make yourself some change, boy. Run this figure over to Big Bob's.

Clement watches Carl take a stubby pencil from his shirt pocket and write on a napkin and wrap three quarters in the paper. As Clement takes the wad of wet napkin and coins and the dime Carl drops in his other hand, he looks for Tommy in the tall stranger's face.

My nephew don't be playing no numbers, Clement. He ain't crazy like the rest of us round here.

Clement felt the man's eyes. They were the eyes of the ghost on Bruston Hill. Eyes that could scream across a room, through a wall. Eyes that could name things when they weren't screaming. Ghost eyes that knew his mother's name.

TOMMY

▼▼▼

Before the dream of his son and the golden, endless beach he had dreamed of Sarah. The kind of dream they say you have when you're drowning, or on a scaffold waiting to be hanged, or blindfolded with your hands tied behind you and your back against a wall. The kind of dream which lets your whole life run like a movie before your eyes, a crowded, sad movie which seems to take forever but starts and ends while the bullets are in the air, while the rope snaps tight, while you fight for one more breath and can't make it and stop fighting the black waves. While he slept on Bruston Hill he watched a dream of his life with Sarah flashing past so it took no time from start to finish, but each image, each memory like a city he could enter and live in forever:

Where have you been? Sarah is sitting on the couch beside the suitcase she had packed a month before. The bag is baby blue, for luck she said when they bought it at Woolworth's, for luck and a healthy baby boy she said while he counted out the nine dollars and ninety-eight cents into her hand. A new bag and everything inside it new. Not for me, she said. For the baby, for our baby to have a fresh start. Her belly has tugged the mini-dress to the tops of her thighs. She looks ready to explode, her stomach twice as big as it had been earlier in the day.

Dammit, man. Where have you been?

You know I been at the pool room.

I called an hour ago. Somebody said you weren't there but would be right back and he said he'd give you the message.

Had to make a little run, Sweetheart. You know. Take care of business. But I'm here, Sugar. Got a cab waiting downstairs.

It's been over an hour.

Nobody told me nothing till a minute ago. Been flying ever since. Take it easy, baby. Get yourself together now. Cab's downstairs with the meter running.

They're coming so fast. Put your hand here. Her stomach hiccups beneath his fingers. The contraction feels like a belch sounds, rippling, a rise and fall, an echo dying in the body's caverns. He stretches his fingers over her roundness, palms her belly like a basketball.

Better get you to the Man. You ready to pop.

Damn the waiting. Damn all the waiting in the world. Sitting on that damned couch scared to death. Scared the baby would start coming and I'd be here all alone and God knows where you were you said you'd be right back you said you'd just be gone a minute.

Then she's talking too much, too loud and moving down the steps too fast for somebody with a belly ready to pop. Heat so heavy in the stairwell it bumps your face. You could make heatballs and bounce them off the sweaty walls. Her voice trails over her shoulder. Telling every nigger in the apartment house their business. The back of her paisley dress is wrinkled, a corner of it folded up above the seat of her panty hose. He wants to smoothe the hem. Wants to dry the sweat blot between her shoulders. He should be in front of her but she's moving too fast. He should be in front to catch her when she comes tumbling down. He tries to grip her elbow, tries to steady her and stop her and tell her to slow down, tell her he loves her and will protect her and love and protect the child she is carrying. He nearly trips himself with the baby blue suitcase. He realizes how high he is when he reaches for her and his hand comes loose and dangles and his fingers close on nothing. Sweat in his eyes. Funky and sweating like a pig. A wrong nigger leaving her alone up all these steps. Alone to carry the baby in the summer heat. No money to go nowhere. Trapped up there in that hot box and him in the street.

Baby, baby. And he wants to tell her he's sorry. Tell her things be better from now on. Be good to her from now on but she is out the front door and the suitcase a dead weight at the end of his arm and his feet aren't moving. He's nailed to one step and she can't hear what he's saying. She's outside yelling at him to come on.

I'm sorry, baby. He wanted to say he was sorry but all that
came out was a big grin as he settled in the cab beside her and
patted her knee. The driver slams the door behind him. A
spasm catches Sarah and drains the blood from her face. He
would kiss her but the tight, thin line of her lips says no. Says
too late. Like kissing a razor he thinks and shoves her new blue
5&10 bag under his knees. He wants to tell her the baby is the
most important thing in the world. Baby wasn't real till Bubba
gave him her message. Then more real than anything and he
hollered and flew out on Frankstown. Almost killed hisself
jumping in front of a cab. Told the driver, I'm having a baby,
man. Laughing and the baby getting more and more real as the
cab raced through the Homewood streets. Wanted to tell her
how scared he got and then the calm flashes when he knew
everything gon be alright. Laughing at hisself because he was
high as a kite. Sitting in that cab he could hear Ruchell tell the
story years later. Your old man was something, boy. Your
pops was a mess. Somebody else chiming in. Yes indeed. Your
daddy flying when you was born, high as John French got on
that Dago Red when his babies came. Old big hat John French
should be here to see it. John French shoulda lived to see these
beautiful grands coming. . . .

Sonny's getting so tall. All that baby fat just melted away.
Tall like his daddy. Got those long hands and long feet like
you.

Yeah, little nigger's growing, sure enough. Supposed to
grow, ain't he? Looked huge first time I seen him after I got
home. She used to bring him in to see me at first. Then she
stopped.

It was hard on Sarah. Just getting out to that prison when
you don't have a car is hard. Hard enough for her, let alone
dragging a baby out there too.

I ain't blaming her. Sometimes I wasn't sure I wanted him
to see me in jail.

I wish you could stay with him now.

Too late, Mama. Ain't no way.

He needs a daddy.

Got a daddy. Just ain't got no home. Home with a righteous
mama and daddy who ain't screaming and fighting all the time.
I tried. Swear to God I tried hard. But it's the same old mess

since I been back. I ain't hitting on nothing. No money. No job. Nothing. What I'm gon do for him or his mama? No point talking bout it. Easier if I just don't see him no more.

Christ looks down from the chapel wall. Long, soft, blond hair like a woman's, a cutie-pie beard, blue eyes painted in a tricky way to stare at you, to follow you around the room, to climb inside your chest. Red letters underneath. *Life Everlasting* in blood red letters. Ain't no red blood in this jive Christ. Kool-aid or Pepsi Cola or some damn thing. This Dude be scared he see Elder Watt knee-walkin cross the bare floor of Tioga Street Sanctified in the Blood of the Lamb Church of God in Christ. When Elder Watt praying and dancing on his old knees you could see that nigger's prayers. See them rise and shimmy and wobble and jerk people out their seats. You could see his prayers camel-walking down the aisle, see them like ladders twisting up in the air. Elder Watt would shout Real, real, Jesus is real. Yes He is now. Real Real. Oh so Real. Real Father Real. Out puffing reefer in the alley, listening to the Saints carry on you could see the walls shake, hear Elder Watt tearing down that raggedy building and putting it together again with real real real, each real a block of shiny stone rising from the ruins.

He hears those prayers, watches his mama's tears because he doesn't shut his eyes. Sneaks looks at everybody else because he doesn't understand what happens when they pray. When he closes his own eyes all he can think of is being old, of smelling old like the people around him on the wooden benches. Powder and perfume and the sweet stuff the men slap on their cheeks after they shave. And the stiff clothes rustling, creaking, the women specially because there are clothes under clothes under clothes and if you ever got to the skin underneath it would be dead because it couldn't breathe. So when you shut your eyes to pray it's like a lid over your head and you think of being old yourself and the people already old are dying and you're trapped there under the lid with the old smells and sweet smells and the stale smell of skin trying to breathe.

He peeks again under the technicolor, tricknicolor eyes of that Christ on Benson's chapel wall. Someone is dead behind all those flowers. His father's father. From the dark side of the family where he got his kinky hair. The short, dark brown man who was Grandpa, who would arrive in his red pickup every

Saturday morning and dig his shaky fingers into his wallet and find *a little something* to help them get through the week. Never stay'd long, just have a cup of coffee if coffee was on and a sweet if they had one in the house.

Don't youall touch that last piece of pie in the icebox. Your grandpa be coming by tomorrow morning. Sometimes the only sweet in the house was the sugar she spooned in his coffee and then they would sit for a few minutes at the kitchen table till whatever made him hurry away each time he visited made him hurry away again.

He was a good man. Don't know what I would have done all those years if he hadn't been there to help out.

Never stayed no time. Always be popping in and popping out.

Mr. Lawson had his ways. He'd never take anything but a cup of coffee and a roll or a piece of cake, something sweet like that if I had it around. On Christmas he'd take a drink. That's why we always kept eggnog. Why I had to fight youall to leave it alone. It was for him. For that eggnog and whiskey he'd take around the holidays. He had his ways and nothing on God's green earth would change him.

Start to fidgeting and you know he's on his way. Stuttering like well . . . well . . . Well I guess I better be movin long.

I asked him to eat with us a thousand times but he was always in a hurry. That's why it seems strange now with him up there so still.

He could deal with them white folks. He was a tough old dude. Taught me how to work when I was little and used to go with him on his truck. Had him a million hustles. Plumbing and roofing and painting and cleaning yards and moving refrigerators. Best job I ever had. Shoot. Only job I ever had where somebody tried to teach me something.

Sarah said she'd be here and bring Sonny.

Better not let her hear you say Sonny. Sarah be bringing Clyde. Her son got him a name, a proper, Christian name. Sarah don't dig no nicknames. All niggers got nicknames. You know. Bumpy Slick Junior Sonny. She won't be bringing no Sonny nowhere.

In his family *Clyde* never had a chance. Everybody made up their own names for a new baby. Clyde was *Sonny* and *Sonny Boy* and *Son Love*. Sonny talking and Sonny Boy walking

and Li'l Son Love got him a toof and Son Son Baby cradled
in somebody's arms *Son son sonny son sonny son son* as somebody made a song of his name and sung Son to sleep.

Don't see him much no more. It's hard but I stay away.

Don't give up so easy. Sarah's a good girl. She waited for
you. She tries hard. Youall talk it over. Try a little harder. I'll
pray for you. Think of Sonny. Think of your boy. I know how
much you love him.

What I'ma do for Sarah. Sarah don't want me hanging
round. Can't do nothing for myself let alone Sarah and Sonny.

He remembers Sarah getting rounder and thicker each day.
When she was carrying Sonny, skinny Sarah was all butt and
belly and breast. She stopped walking and started to move like
a boat. Not waddle like a duck like he thought she would but
roll easy through a room like the room was water and she was
one of those sailing ships easing through it. Trying to tell her
all the time she was looking good. Tried to play around with
her, but she didn't like it said she was a balloon and he had
the string in his hand and she didn't like it cause he could just
let go if he got tired holding it.

She is at the door of the chapel, her eyes lowered to the
visitors' book like she is looking for a secret in there or like
she doesn't know what to write. Like she doesn't know if she
is Sarah this or Sarah that because the string is broken and
there she stands looking at the book with Sonny in her arms.
And that little dude's already too big to carry. Looks long as
his mother.

Then he is beside them and says Hey and reaches out to
touch them but Sarah tightens her grip and the boy buries his
face deeper into her cold-stiffened coat.

Say hello to your father, Clyde.

He is his father so he leans his face closer, nuzzling, nibbling
till a smile dimples the plump, cold cheeks. He is closer to her
also, closer to the little hovering Sarah cloud and it surrounds
him, perfume and cinnamon breath, the bones under her clothes
rustling brittle from the cold.

Shouldn't be smiling. Even the baby shouldn't be smiling.
Not here. Nothing here but long faces and walking like you
on eggs. Got that organ on tape. Precious Lord Take My Hand.
But all the songs the same. Playing long face and creeping
round like your feet might hurt Benson's floor. Like you ain't
good enough to be alive. Like you supposed to be sorry you

breathing. Precious Lord Take My Hand. He wanted to stop
it. Tear the speaker from the wall. Stomp its dusty face. Snatch
the little man inside and smash his brains out against the grinning teeth of the keyboard. The music had nothing to do with
his dead grandfather. Nothing to do with life but it dogged his
steps as he followed Sarah and his son down an aisle into the
chapel.

Sonny slides from Sarah's arms, bounces a moment on
Benson's pearl grey rug then hugs his grandmother's legs before
she sweeps him up and his knees land in her lap. She wraps
her arms around him and pulls him to her chest and rocks him
as she rocks herself side to side on the funeral parlor chair.
Not rocking to the organ. She's down with Elder Watt rocking
on the bare boards. Her face shines over the boy's shoulder.
Bright tears, glad tears as she rises to higher ground. Her face
in two places at once. Worry lines, age lines say his mother's
on the bench beside him. But her eyes are gone, lifted to the
higher ground. She wants to take Sonny with her. Rocks him
back and forth. Her shoulders sway, circle, wing her to the
higher ground.

Think of Sonny. Think of your boy.

He has seen his mother's face cry and laugh like that when
he opened his eyes to watch the others pray. Like she has him
in her arms again. Like she's pressing him to her bosom and
squeezing and he can't hardly breathe. Sonny in her arms now,
but he's rocking there too. Spying on people's faces while they
sing and pray. When her heart opens you could fall in. Sonny
squirms, pulls away, big-eyed like he's scared. Like he's in
a hurry to find Sarah.

Then they playing keep-away. Sonny pulled from one
woman's lap to another. Passed over him like he ain't there.
Like he's monkey in the middle.

I didn't know whether to come. But Mr. Lawson loved
Clyde. And he did everything he could to help us. I thought
we both should be here.

Of course you should be here.

Talking over him now. Like he ain't there. Like he's monkey
in the middle and keep away.

I hoped you'd feel that way.

He'd want you both here. He was a proud man. He'd want
you to see him this way the last time. Benson did a good job.
He knew he better. Mr. Lawson picked out the casket and the

room, the suit he's wearing, everything he wanted, and paid
Benson a long time ago. Knew if he want it done right, he
better do it hisself. He knew his people. Knew they'd be squabbling over that little bit of insurance money and Benson get it
all. He knew his people. Knew us all. Me. You. Sonny.
Tommy. Knew us all.

Mr. Lawson never called him Sonny.

No. He knew you. Knew how people get a thing about
names. That's why he was always Mister Lawson to me. Never
thought of calling him anything else. He always called Tommy,
Thomas Edgar. Never just Thomas or Tommy but Thomas
Edgar. Said the white man used to call us whatever he wanted.
Uncle and Cuffy and Boy. Anything came into their heads. But
now we got real names, *entitles* he said, and if man got a
name nobody had a right to call him out his name. He said he
fought all his life for a name.

Well, this one will be Clyde as long as I'm around.

Youall talking a lot of trash. Nothing wrong with Sonny.
Things different now. This is a new day now. I mean I can
call my son what I want to. I mean Sonny just as *respectable*
as Clyde if I'm the one saying Sonny. I mean I'm his daddy
and not some jive white man come along calling him out his
name.

You don't see Clyde for weeks at a time. He doesn't see
you and doesn't get one red cent from you. Don't sit here
talking about your rights. Daddy's just a word. This child can't
eat it, he can't wear it, he can't run to it when he wakes up
crying in the middle of the night.

My Grandpa's up there in that casket so I ain't gon tell you
what I'm thinking. Maybe I ain't even got a right to think what
I'm thinking but anyway I sure ain't saying nothing with him
up there. This is his show so I'm just gon sit and respect the
dead.

I'm sorry.

I'm sorry too. So sorry I wish I knew a word worse than
sorry. . . .

Sarah with Sonny sleeping in her lap is framed in the rearview mirror of his brother's car. He is driving and has to ask
her for directions. Away less than a year and the streets had
changed. Streets dying, streets blocked, streets made into One
Ways, streets gouged out in the middle, streets where the trolley

tracks were being ripped from their cobbled beds. Streets going in circles and streets where no cars were allowed. In jail he had depended upon a dream of those streets, a dream in which they never changed their shape, the life in them remaining the same till he returned. Kept a picture of the streets in his mind. Tioga Dumferline Susquehanna Homewood Hamilton Frankstown Finance a picture frozen like before a commercial on TV. And the streets, the life in the streets would wait for him to return and then everything be moving, everything be just as he left it. Moving again, alive again because he was back. Tioga Dumferline Susquehanna. The shortest way between places not a question of walking but a matter of being in one place and thinking he wanted to be in another and dreaming the flow of the streets unfurling behind him, beside him till he got where he wanted to go. Gliding from the corner of Frankstown and Homewood, from Bubba's pool room to home. Close his eyes and it happened. Three blocks on Homewood, cut down Hamilton where the trolleys used to run and after two blocks cross over the bumpy street, the tracks which used to guide number 76 to the streetcar barn four blocks farther on from where he crosses over Hamilton to Dumferline. Dumferline a short narrow street where Willy Meadows lived and you don't have to stop and kick his butt because he's dead of an overdose and Willy don't wait anymore in his front window sticking his tongue out when you pass so you don't have to try and sneak up on him one of those days when he's playing on the sidewalk and kick his butt you just go on past the little, green-roofed, leaning Meadows house till Dumferline dies at Tioga which you cross catty-corner to pick up an alley called Cassina Way and Cassina is the last street you're on till the dirt alley where you cut left and come to your back door.

That's how you do it. In his cell he'd dream the streets gliding past perfect in each detail. The music at the record store, the fried chicken and fried fish smell of Hot Sauce William's Bar–B–Que, the blinking red and yellow lights you pay no attention to at intersections. Ghosts of trolley cars make the wires sing over your head. He kept the streets inside him. Even though they were full of broken glass, and cracks, the garbage stacked at the curbs and boards over the empty windows and iron cages over the windows with anything in them, and black stones still smelling of smoke, still smelling of dead winos and dead firemen in the vacant lot after they tried to burn down the

streets one hot August night. Even though he left little bloody
pieces of himself scattered all over the streets, he kept the
dream. Frozen storefronts and frozen faces and music frozen
in the darkness of his cell.

In the rearview mirror Sarah's face. She looks out the window. Not a girl anymore. Not a pretty girl face like a flower
nobody ever touched. Soft girl face gone but she was Sarah,
the mother of his son, the wife lost like everything else lost
because he was evil and cold just like they always said. Good
for nothing like they said. A cold evil nigger killing her girl
face, burning it up the way they burnt up Homewood Avenue.

He had stood beside her on burlap at the edge of the fresh
grave. The drivers from Benson's held the coffin on straps over
the mouth of a gaping hole. The earth was freshly turned and
loose under his feet even though everywhere else the ground
was frozen. He had let his eyes run over the faces of the
mourners. Like Sunday in the Homewood A.M.E.Z. Church.
His Grandpa had no church so they buried him out of Homewood, Reverend Harrison presiding. In limousines from Benson's to the church, the pallbearers in white gloves so thin you
could see the black of their hands through the material. He
didn't want to be a pallbearer. Didn't want to touch the handles
of the coffin. Always been afraid of dead things. No matter
how small, how dead, and it was a dead man in the box.
Limousines from the church to the cemetery and since the dead
man was his Grandpa, he'd go this once all the way with him.
Go with his son and Sarah since he knew they too needed to
go. So he stood on the burlap over the freshly turned earth and
stole the faces of the mourners while their eyes were closed
and they prayed and chanted their last good-byes.

Yea though I walk through the Valley of the Shadow. Yea
though I walk. The voices drift up the hillside, lost in the
stillness of brown earth and bare trees. Like a mighty trumpet
in Homewood A.M.E. Zion but here under an iron January sky
their voices a kind of lost whisper gone before it got started.
Sarah's lips formed the words of a prayer but she didn't say
it. Just her breath twisting like smoke in the cold air. The words
unspoken, dying in warm balloons of air as her lips opened
and closed in time with the preacher. In his cell he had tried
to put together her face. The feathery lashes, her skin taut over
high cheekbones, the brown clean sweep of forehead from her
dark brows to the dark tangle of her hair. Wanted her to be

like the Homewood streets so he could shut his eyes and slip from place to place, so he could hold her safe inside, so she would be there ready to come to life again when he returned. But he couldn't do it, couldn't find her face the way it was when she was sleeping, the way it was when he'd wake up first and look over at her and forget for a moment the empty day on its way. In her sleeping face he could lose himself. Forget who he'd been, what he was, because she was beautiful and peaceful and for a while nothing else counted. He would raise the covers and look down at her naked body and it would take his breath away because each time it would be like seeing her the first time, the darker brown circles on her breasts, the breasts like eyes seeing through him and around him. A stranger's mysterious body nestled warm and soft beside him and he'd need her, want her but wouldn't say a word, wouldn't break the charm because then the day would start, he'd lose the magic in her sleeping body. In jail she kept moving, turning away, pulling the covers tight around her body, hissing at him for breaking her sleep. He saw the bits and pieces of her spinning, out of focus, a breast, a hand, a thigh pulling away, resisting, hiding itself and the ache in his groin would mount to his throat and the bitter *not taste* of her would be dry in his mouth. And his hands would pull and stroke and tear at his own flesh because he could not bear the raw emptiness they grasped when she would not stay still in his dream.

Sarah still now, praying silently beside the open grave, lost to the son beside her who fidgeted with the folds of her coat. His son who would never know the man Benson's people were lowering into the earth, his son who would never know the man whose cold evil shadow shivered on the burlap behind him.

Sarah sitting in the back seat of his brother's car so Sonny could stretch out and rest. She rides a vacant stare out the back window and he wonders what she sees in the battered streets. In the Homewood streets so changed in a year he had to ask her directions twice just getting from the cemetery to where she lived.

He sleep?

I think so.

He alright?

It's been a long morning for a little boy. He was upset by people crying. He didn't understand.

What you tell him?

I told him Grandpa had gone away and we wouldn't see him anymore. Clyde called him Grandpa like you did.

Yeah.

You know how smart Clyde is. Nothing gets past him. He knows something terrible has happened. He's been very quiet and sticking closer to me than usual.

Shoulda told him Grandpa's dead. Dead and gone.

Don't let's talk about it. He may be listening. He doesn't miss much.

Kelley Street is one-way now, a wasteland for two blocks after Braddock. Like it's been bombed. All the houses knocked down, snow-cluttered piles of plaster, bricks and lathe boards. Rotten beams jutting from basement cavities into which houses were bulldozed. The third block, seventy-four hundred, had been spared. Bright pink and green and blue, the freshly painted rowhouses grinned at him like somebody with new false teeth. Sarah's is a green one, seventy-four-fifteen. He found a space where the broken curbstone would not scrape the car doors when they opened. The bundle of Sonny lifted out and tucked in one arm, the free hand reaching back into the car for Sarah's, which it brushes for a moment, but she is pushing her black dress down over her knees and scooting to the edge of the seat and out on her own two feet, her heels clacking on the pavement, her long legs briskly scissoring to the green door. Sonny should be heavier in his arms, but the boy is losing his lumpy baby weight, his arms and legs are stretching out. His son's bones drape across his chest, a cling, a lean, a dangle to his body, his son beginning to learn to carry his own weight even while he is held in someone's arms.

On the golden beach again and a blood red sun hangs half in the sky, half hidden beneath the sea so the rippling surface of the water from his eyes to the horizon is on fire. He looks back at their tracks in the wet sand. They stretch undisturbed, paralleling the curving shoreline as far as he can see. The tracks are puddles and in those closest he can see bubbles and shifting sand, new life being freed where they have stepped. Sonny's hand is cool and warm in his. He laughs and lets go his son and starts to run. Giant, high-kneed strides like Jim Brown and O.J. jitterbugging in and out of the waves, up and back from the breakers to the sand, dodging, shifting, always escaping the rushing sea swells riding up the beach. Sonny is clapping and laughing too. Watching his daddy zigzagging and high stepping and whooping and free as a bird.

Sarah had been his woman and Sonny would always be his son and he wanted to feel good about entering this green-doored cardboard house where they lived. It still smelled of fresh paint. He recognizes a few pieces of furniture, the rug from their old apartment. He wonders if she kept the king-size bed, the bed where the three of them had slept, where he watched Clyde drinking from Sarah's breasts, her milk-swollen breasts as strange and new as the baby.

Clyde learned to crawl on this rug under his feet. Sarah had wanted something soft and warm, a thick pile rug to hide the cracked floorboards of their apartment, a rug to cut the drafts and cushion the baby's falls. So he lied about having a job and got instant credit and signed a note and promised to pay three times what the carpet was worth so he could get it delivered the same day he scratched his name on the paper. He bought the rug at the jacked-up instant credit price and received the free bonus of a wall clock. Neither rug nor clock worked. Sarah used to borrow a vacuum cleaner from her mother. He could see her rocking back and forth, her robe flapping open at each stroke because that watermelon starting to grow and nothing on underneath the robe but skin and the dark hair between her legs. Stroking back and forth, combing the nappy rug. He hears the noisy vacuum she had to cart up all those stairs, sees her naked legs as she sways and the robe parts to her waist and her arm pushes up and back, up and back but the rug always looked like a mangy dog needing a bath. Not four years old yet, he could date it by Sonny's age, but the nappy motherfucker looked a hundred. He wondered if Sarah had ever finished the payments. One day he burned all the bills. Crumbled them and threw them in the sink and burned the mothers just like they had burned half of Homewood Avenue one summer night. He parted the beige fibers of the rug with his toe, exposing the network of grey threads anchoring the tufts. He remembered the balding head of the Jew who sold him the rug and kicked deeper into the bare patch.

Sarah had carried Sonny upstairs. A kettle hummed in the kitchen. When he had that janitor's job for a couple of weeks Sarah would wake up with him at 3:00 A.M. and they'd sit half sleep at the kitchen table waiting for the pig-nosed kettle to whistle. The hum was rising to a high-pitched whine when he lifted the kettle, the same red kettle with the black snout, from the burner. There were clean cups and silverware in a plastic rack beside the sink, a jar of instant coffee on the countertop. Easy to find sugar in the bare cupboards and he was dumping a second spoonful into a cup when Sarah came down the steps.

Like old times.

Thanks for catching the pot. I forgot I turned on the stove and that noise would have waked Clyde for sure.

How long you been here?

A month or so.

Mama said something bout you moving but never said where. Been meaning to get your address. You know. In case something comes up. In case I get my hands on a little something to send you.

I still take my mail at my mother's. They steal it here. Junkies go through the boxes. I know they get in the house when I go out. But there's nothing worth stealing. I used to be afraid to open my own door, afraid I'd catch one in here and he'd get scared and hurt me or hurt the baby. Don't know why they waste their time searching these shacks. The people in them poor as everybody else around here. Still when I come home after dark, if the light's on next door I ask one of the fellas who live there to come with me while I go through the rooms and turn on my lights. They think I'm crazy.

Coulda stayed at your mother's.

I need my privacy. Anyway we're doing alright here. Just have to get used to being on my own.

Sonny sleep?

I think so. He was whimpering when I put him down. Didn't hear anything before I came back downstairs. He should be tired, but he's a little scared.

Shoulda told him I'm here.

Sleep's what he needs. And a little time to get himself together. He doesn't need any more excitement. He doesn't see you for weeks at a time and he just gets confused.

Shoulda told him Grandpa's dead and done. Shoulda told him his daddy's here.

Daddy's just a word when there's no man around.

That what you tell Sonny?

I tell Clyde the truth.

Like what truth? Like your truth? Like he ain't got no daddy?

Don't get started. And don't raise your voice. He needs

sleep. He's too young to deal with all this. I'm his mother,
I'm grown and I can't deal with it. Your grandfather was a
good man. He helped any way he could and never asked for
a thing in return. I hated to see him just shrivel up the way he
did. Lying in a hospital bed getting more and more helpless.
I had to stop going to see him. Couldn't look him in the face.
It was just too pitiful. Half the time he wouldn't even know
if anybody was in the room with him. So I stayed away. Then
I got ashamed to go back because I had stayed away too long.
I knew he'd be mad and fuss at me and I wouldn't have an
answer. He did so much. Everything he could. Even when he
got too old and sick to work he shared the little bit he had.

Bone and blood in the back of his hand. Bones and bloodlines from his grandfathers. One white as a white man. Grandpa
a dark spot in the snapshots in Geraldine's book. John French
fairskinned and tall and lanky till he got old and got that belly.
Harry Lawson a shortish, dark, thick-chested man till they took
him in the hospital and he had them operations and they start
chopping chunks of that solid, dark meat off his bones so by
the end nothing to him, by the end wasn't nothing under his
hospital gown but feathers and bone. Feathers and bone the
time he helped the nurse move him so she could straighten his
bed. Like not so much a question of getting his Grandpa's
weight up in his arms as it was a matter of holding him tight,
circling the feathers and bone with his arms so the old man
wouldn't fly away.

John French would throw him in the air. He wore a big hat
and drank wine and chewed tobacco. He was a gambling man
they said. A rogue they say and taught him nasty songs which
made the women say, Hush up boy, don't you ever let me hear
you say that nastiness again. And say to his grandfather, Why
you teach that child something like that? And John French
would roll. He'd slap his knees and laugh and choke till he
coughed tobacco juice in the brass bowl sat by his armchair.
He had grown up in John French's house. His mother and
father separated for the first time and his mother had no place
to go but back to her father's house on Cassina Way with the
children. The best time of his life. Cousins from up on Bruston
Hill to play with, the house full of aunts and him the youngest,
the spoiled darling. Then it all went to pieces when John French
died. When he died in the bathroom and they couldn't get his
big body unwedged from the bathtub and the toilet and the

women had to get help and Fred Clark came and everybody
screaming and finally they got him laid out across the bed but
he was gone and it all went to pieces. There were places in
that old house he could never touch again. The places where
John French had been dead. Places he still didn't go in now.

It's a bitch out here. I mean the world don't make no sense.
I got two grandfathers, right? A black one and a white one.
And both them die the same day. Same goddamned day sev-
enteen years apart. December 29. And my birthday the 28th.
Now what kind of sense does that make?

And what kind of sense it make for me to be sitting here?
Loved you and loved that boy more than anything. But I
wouldn't do right. Just couldn't do right to save my soul. Love
him and love you and here I sit like some goddamn stranger
drinking coffee at your table. He had to die to get us in the
same room. Now what kind of sense that make?

It's too late. I'm sorry but it's too late. You don't know
who Clyde is, and he surely doesn't know you. If you had
stayed with him, with us . . . maybe. But you're a stranger now
and it'd just confuse him. Dealing with you here today and
then dealing with you gone again tomorrow. You're the nice
man he calls Daddy and you bring candy when you come and
you tickle him and throw him up in the air and catch him and
he watches TV with you till way after his bedtime but that's
all there is to it.

Go away. Don't be beating around the goddamned bush.
For once in your life say something loud and clear. Say *Go
away, jive nigger.* Say it loud and clear.

You're already away. You've been away since before he
was born.

Don't start no mess.

I'm tired. I don't want to go through it ever again. Not your
little business you always had to leave and take care of, not
your lies, not Ruchell and those tacky, junkie whores youall
ran with. None of it. That's the past. It's over and done. I
thought I had a man but I didn't. I know it now when I stand
there afraid to open my own front door. I know it when I have
to ask strangers to go in my house and scare away the ghosts.
I know it when I have to put a coffee pot on the stove so it will
whistle and I won't be alone. Forget it. I know where it's at.
And so does he.

He always be my son.

You're the one fucked him in me. That's all.

Don't start talking shit. Ain't ready for no shit today.

I'm not ready either. I'm sad and I'm hurt and I'm scared and I don't have room to feel sorry for you. I don't have the words, I don't have the time to deal with you. You always needed somebody to feel sorry for you. You always need somebody to forgive you. Maybe that's why you did so much wrong. So somebody could feel sorry, so somebody could forgive.

Look here. I ain't asking for nothing. You can get up off my case. I ain't come here for no bad mouth from you. Can't be in the same room five minutes without nastiness going back and forth.

It's all there is between us.

Sonny's upstairs, woman. Wasn't for me he wouldn't be here. Ain't much but it's something. Say what you want about me. I'm still his daddy. I was a wrong nigger. Sometimes I knew I was fucking up and sometimes I didn't know. Sometimes I cared about fucking up and sometimes I didn't give a damn. Now that's a wrong nigger. That's me and I'm dealing with that. Got to deal with it. Look back sometimes and I want to cry. But I ain't crying. No time to cry. Don't do no good no way. Then I get mad. The shit comes down heavy on me. Don't care what happens. Don't care about nothing. Nobody gives a shit and neither do I.

I'm sorry. I really am. Sorry for us both. We didn't make it. But now you've gone your way and I'm trying to make a life for Clyde. You can't come back whenever you're in the mood and put us through changes. You had your chance for a son but you didn't want him. You wanted the street, whatever you loved so much in those gutter-rotten streets, and that's what you choose and that's what you got. It's too late now.

Bones and bloodlines. Wonders why the back of his hand don't blow apart. He gripped the hard edge of the plastic countertop. Why don't his veins split and the black blood and the white blood of his grandfathers spurt up like a fountain. If he sat still any longer he would explode. She had said he loved the streets and he could remember times when he screamed freedom, he needed his freedom, he needed to get out of the house and be free. Was that what he loved? Was that what the pounding in his head and the bulging veins in his hands were saying now? What was there inside him that needed to be free?

What was there inside him so strong that it made him turn his back on Sarah and turn his back on his son, so strong it could split open his skin?

He got up and left Sarah alone at the table staring into her coffee. He passed the steps and walked toward the curtained front window. Other men walk through these rooms, other men stop at the stairs and smile and climb to her bedroom. To the king-size bed nobody had ever paid for. But it's her bed now. And her son.

He parted the green drapes and watched Kelley Street. You can get to Homewood A.M.E. Zion by walking down Kelley. Not this end of Kelley where Sarah lived but the other part below Braddock was one way of going from home to church. No one walking now. Only a dog across the street at the end of the pastel rowhouses up on its hind legs worrying a garbage can lid. The sky greyer and greyer. Perhaps it would snow again. What color was a sky when it was fixing to snow? Did the greyness get closer, lower? Was it mixed with white? Had anybody ever watched close enough, long enough to know? Did the sky always look this weary when people died? Was it like this seventeen years ago when they buried John French? Will people stand on burlap to keep their feet clean when they bury him? Will Sonny be peeking, stealing the faces of the mourners?

The pool room a fifteen-minute walk from Sarah's. The Brass Rail ten. Homewood distances measured in foot time because he'd never had a car. He would tell Sonny what the boy needed to know. What everybody needed to know.

Will you look at that sky. Look at that gold fire on the water. You could march cross the ocean if you got feet like those black Indins walk on hot coals.

Daddy, what is dying?

Dying's what we all got to do someday.

When?

You know not the hour. That's what the song says.

Why?

Cause it happens to everything. Trees, birds, people. Everything got to have a beginning. And if it got a beginning, it's got to have a middle and then it's got to end. People start by being born. Like you was, out your beautiful mama, Sarah. People live and that's the middle. Dying is the end. Even mountains have to die.

Will I die?

Don't have to be worrying about dying for a long time. You just got started, little man.

Will you die?

When my time comes.

Will it come before I die?

Nobody knows. But you just beginning. You probably be around long after I'm dead and gone.

I don't understand. I don't like it, Daddy.

Death's a mystery. Life's a mystery. Your cousin Kaleesha only here a few days. Don't seem to make no sense, do it? Don't nobody understand much bout any of it, you get right down to it. Just hold my hand. Look at that sky. Look at that burning water. Ain't it a sight?

But what is death?

Death's like . . . it's like being gone forever.

For a long, long, long, long time.

Long like that, but even longer. Dead people go away and they never come back.

Where do they go?

They go . . . to the sky . . . to the earth. Different people believe different things. A song I like says *To My Father's House.* Old folks say *Over Jordan.* And songs say other things too. One say *One More River To Cross.* One say *There's A Home Far Beyond the Blue.* Another just say *Farther Along.* Used to hear all them old songs on Sunday morning. Your Grammy Lizabeth always had gospel on the radio. Sometimes the songs made her cry. Sometimes she'd shout Amen, or Hallelujah. Scared me sometimes cause she seem far away. Had to touch her and make sure she still standing in the kitchen fixing breakfast or ironing shirts.

I don't want to go away. I don't want you to go away. I'm scared, Daddy.

And he was two people walking along the beach with his son. Two so one could grip the boy's hand tighter and be scared himself but the other him could sing those old songs and dance on the waves and think of something to make the boy laugh. The other person he was could hear the sea gulls chattering like kids playing jumprope in the playground and make up a nasty rhyme to chant to the rhythm of the turning rope. A rhyme funny and nasty so the boy would laugh because he knew he was getting away with something when the women shushed him and wagged their fingers and fussed at whoever taught him such terrible mess.

Two so he could see the man and boy and the footprints and the crimson sea and sky. So the dream could turn happy again and the stories the man told the boy come true again, someplace, somewhere. On the other side of the green curtain.

The stairwell in this house on Kelley is narrow. It stinks of raw paint and shellac. Wood squeaks no matter how softly he plants his feet. He is following the trail of Sarah's lover up the stairs, following a dude who smells barbershop clean, who's sharp as a tack, a dude with a job and a new ride, a dude who could do something for Sarah and Sonny. A dude whose new shoes squeak, who goes to the left at the head of the stairs, left to the open bedroom and the king-size bed with its fancy spread. But he goes right, toward the peedy smell leaking into the hallway. He takes his first deep breath since he entered the house. What he's been trying to hold in, sighs out. Pee stings his nostrils.

Sonny's breathing is loud, ragged. It sputters inside his stuffy nostrils. Sonny still wetting his bed. Too old for that. And too young to be standing outdoors in raw weather beside a raw grave so the chill and dampness turn to a frozen puddle inside his body. Snuffling and sneezing and a runny nose. Why is Sonny wetting his bed like a baby?

He pushes the cracked door inward. Grey light leans against Sonny's face. He was sleeping on his side, on the bed near the door, only his face uncovered and one arm dangling from beneath the quilt. He holds his breath and steps through the opening. His shadow crosses the shaft of grey light, crosses Sonny's face. When he reaches the bed, the full-size bed on which the boy's body is barely a lump, he stands aside to let the dull glow from the open door fall again on Sonny's features. Sonny's lips hang open, twitch, are purple in the gloom. His daddy's full lips, heavy eyebrows and lashes, Sarah's fair skin, her delicate, curving neck, her high cheekbones. The boy's face helpless as a mirror. Rattling sighs fill the room. Somewhere in the darkness was a pile of wet, pee-soaked clothes. And his son too old for that. Something wrong to make him still do that.

I hope you didn't wake him. He needs his sleep.

He's sleep. Ain't got nothing to say anyway. Just wanted

to see him and let him see me. But he's sleep. What I got to say anyway? Just out here in the street is all. That's all I know. Nothing. How to get over on nothing. Just out in the street hustling to stay alive. So what I got to say to him?

When my other grandfather John French died it just about killed me. Sick for days. Couldn't go to the funeral or nothing. Nobody never told me nothing bout dying. A baby like Sonny but I remember saying to myself over and over, Why didn't nobody tell me bout this? Why didn't they tell me? Nobody said Boo, and then him gone and then nothing nobody could tell me make no difference. Keep seeing this big hole in the middle of John French's house, in the middle of everything and he fell in and anybody could fall in and nobody never said a mumbling word about it till too late.

Then his arms are around Sarah, and the grey sky, the grey light of the streets, the grey light spreading across the floor of Sonny's room are in her eyes. Her brown eyes glazed by grey rain, by slants of grey rain like the bars of a cage. And the bars are steel and he reaches through them to cup her face in his hands, her face which fits the heart shape of his empty hands grabbing through the bars. But she won't stay still. The room goes out of focus as he buries his head on her shoulder, in the Sarah cloud of perfume and cinnamon breath and bones rustling. His hands are busy finding her body under the silky black dress, the deep curve of her back, the springy strength under satin skin. He is saying her name. Breathing *Sarah* into her shoulder. His hands are shaping the word as they slip over the outline of her panties, as they ride the swell of her hips and squeeze the firm flesh. He sees her robe surrender to the bump of her watermelon belly, the blue robe open up to her waist, her belly pouting above her naked legs. He is whispering her name into her ear. Sarah, Sarah. Drawing her closer and tightening the circle of his arms.

Till he hears what she is saying. Till he feels the iron in her shoulders. Her arms bent at the elbow were drawn up like sticks between them. He hears her asking why. Why, Why, Why, as she pushes him away.

No. Not this way.

Sarah.

No . . .

Sarah.

We're just feeling sorry for ourselves. I needed somebody's shoulder to cry on. I thought that's what you needed. But you want more. You want everything.

Hey, girl.

Why?

It's me, baby. It's me. Don't it feel good? Don't it feel right? It's me, baby. I need you.

That's not enough.

What you talking bout? Don't talk.

There's tomorrow and yesterday. There's all the lies. All the hardness. All the days I've spent getting together the little bit I could to make a new life. All the things I can't understand about you and never will till the day I die.

He rehearses all the pleas he could make. His gift of words. His rap. His jive, the old front porch, vestibule, couch, door-way, backyard, backseat, Westinghouse Park game he always won. He thought of all the times he'd gotten over, all the raps to all the chicks, and the words churned in his guts like food gobbled down too fast. The grey rain had passed. Everything in the room sharply in focus. He was as naked as the bare walls and his hands had no right being anyplace but at the ends of his arms. His hands hung through the bars, limp, dead, raw from grasping nothing.

There was a time he would have sung to her. Tenor lead of the Commodores down on one knee. *Why do you have to go? The night is still young yet.* Fling his cape over his shoulder like the Count of Monte Cristo, the Duke of Earl, Speedo and the rest of those bad motherfuckers and be chirping and be down and coming on so heavy what else she gon do but get up off some trim, Jack. There was a time. But she won't stand still and all the words from all the songs are smoke in his mouth, are bitter in his throat and he can't even say one word, make one sound but the screaming deep inside, the scream of his hands as they shake the iron bars of his cell.

Sarah.

Yes, yes, yes, Son. That's how you began. Inside your beautiful mama, Sarah. Swimming round in there like a little goldfish, jumping round in there like Froggy the Gremlin and I could feel your little frog legs through your mama's skin and see her belly jump when you hopping round in there. That's the beginning, you're just getting started so don't worry none. Don't you know Froggy went a courtin and he did ride Uh huh, uh huh. Right on down to Miss Mousey's house. Uh huh. And don't you know the goose drank Thunderbird wine and the monkey chewed Five Brother's tobacco on number 88 trolley car line. And don't you know there's black Indins don't feel pain in they feet. They could walk on that burning water all the way out to where you see the sun taking a bath. Now ain't that something? Ain't that a good something to know?

BESS

▼▼▼

Don't nobody set foot inside here but that boy, Clement, who runs to the store for me. He gets me what I need from down the hill and he probably be the one find me dead in here one of these mornings he knocks and I don't answer the door. Some of them used to come up here call theyselves keeping an eye on me but I stop em at the door now. Ain't none their business what I'm doing I been on this earth long before most them even thought of so I stop em now they don't get past the porch now I say what you want or say go away and don't even open the door so they don't bother me no more. That boy's the only one I see regular and he's the only one sets his foot inside my door.

It was your sister, Lizabeth's middle child, the one they call Shirl she one of the last I let in here. Favors her mama and her mama's the image of Freeda, my sister's girl. Freeda was the oldest and the prettiest in her quiet way. But don't you let those quiet ways fool you. She run away with John French quiet enough didn't she? So quiet she fooled everybody till she come back four days later and told Bill Campbell, I'm married. I'm married now. And she was married good. You know John French married her good. Quiet as she was she was married good and you could see the brazen in her eyes you never saw before when she come back after four days talking about she's married to that rogue John French.

She's the one. The one they call Shirl. Don't tell me I don't know youall. I know just who you are. Wrapped up like some Indin Chief in my blanket. Snoring like a hog at my table. I thought you saying something to me and I turns around and what is it? It's you snoring like a hog and I got my mouth open like a fool to answer you.

She sat right where you're sitting. Had that baby with her.

128

Carried that baby all the way up Bruston Hill and that's why
I let her in. Summertime too so you know she had to have
something on her mind to tote that baby on her back all the
way up this wicked hill. Well she said, Hi Mother Bess. Said
I brought the baby to see you, Mother Bess. I was on the porch
in my rocking chair like I usually be and I had to squint the
sweat out my eyes before I could see good who was talking
at me. Then I saw Gert. Then I saw Freeda. Then I saw Lizabeth. Then I saw the one they call Shirl with this little brown
baby in a sack on her back. That's the way they do nowadays.
Carry they children like wild Indins. And that's how I heard
Sybela Owens brought them babies from slavery. Had a sling
crost her back and brought them all the way from slavery to
the top of this hill. So I'm rubbing sweat out my eyes and
trying to see who I see because I get to rocking in that old chair
and mize well be blind as Sybela Owens, mize well have that
black cape she always wore draped over my eyes cause I ain't
seeing nothing outside, ain't studying nothing but what I keeps
inside and that sure ain't nobody's business and I'll tell em in
a minute go on away from here go on and leave me alone.

She said Hi and I said Come on up here and bring that baby
out the sun, girl. Cause now I could see that's what it was. A
baby back there like them Indins call papoose and she been
totin it all the way up Bruston Hill on her back in the broiling
sun. Poor little thing probably bar–b–qued back there and I'm
wondering if this girl got good sense and wondering what she
got on her mind, if she got a mind, climbing Bruston Hill like
that.

She sat at the table where you're sitting and drank a glass
of this nasty nail-tasting water. Tried to cut it for her but she
said No thanks and drank it warm as pie and nasty as it is right
out the spigot. Fed the baby out a bottle she had tucked back
there with it in the sack. Cute, chubby-legged, little chocolate
brown baby. She was wearing a cap to keep the sun out her
face and the little thing sweating like a horse under that cap.
A whole headful of hair. Looked like a wet chicken all sweated
up under that cap. That's your daddy's side of the family.
Nothing but good hair on your mama's side. All of us Hollin-
gers had that long straight hair. Was a time I could sit on mine.
And Freeda too when she married John French had that good
hair all the way down her back. But this dimple brown little
thing look like a drowned hen till her mama dried it and combed

it out nice and plaited it again and fixed five or six of them teensy barrettes in .there. Said she was Kaleesha and I said what'd you say and she said that African-sounding name again and I said I thought that's what you said and didn't say Why you go and name a child something like that. Kept my big mouth shut for once and said it *Kaleesha* out loud cause it wasn't none of my business. Kaleesha. And the little thing smiled up at me out the biggest, prettiest black eyes I ever seen. Yes they was now. The prettiest I've seen and I've seen many an eye in my day but these was the brightest and blackest and prettiest. Didn't matter they rolled around and crossed sometimes. They was the prettiest black-eyed Susan black eyes under that fuzzy head and I can see them today just as plain as I seen them when she was sitting on her mama's lap right where you sitting.

That's why I went down this hill one last time when they told me she died. Don't know which one it was come up here to tell me cause I didn't open the door but I heard alright and it shocked my nerves. All I could think of the rest of the day was them eyes. Brown as she was and fuzzy-headed too and chubby-cheeked like babies supposed to be I could see her mama in her face and if her mama was there in that baby face you know I seen Gert and Lizabeth and Freeda. Whoever it was on my porch knocking then talking through the door then getting huffy cause I wouldn't let him in. Said they'd bury her on Wednesday and somebody be by in the morning to take me down. Didn't pay no mind to all those words. Heard him talking and heard him getting mad cause I didn't answer but I wasn't studying him or studying no funeral or no Wednesday or nothing else because them big black eyes was in this room and I said Jesus and said Good God Almighty because that's what I say when there ain't nothing else to say even though I ain't been a Christian for years, Jesus and Good God Almighty cause what else you gon say when some old woman ninety-nine hundred years old still living and breathing on the top of this hill and that little baby's gone. I ain't got no life no more I'm just puttering around here waiting to die but that child's dead and I got them eyes, them pretty baby black wandering eyes floating round here.

I let them take me. Let them talk that Mother Bess this and Mother Bess that foolishness and kissed the children they pushed in my face. They think that's good luck. They think

I'm mean enough and crazy enough and old enough to have
some kind of power so they bring the little ones and push em
up in my face. That's why she climbed Bruston Hill with her
baby on her back. Climbed up here in all that sunshine and sat
where you're sitting and cried at my table. Cause the doctors
had give up. They named it then they give up. Some terrible
name. Couldn't nobody but the doctors say the name of that
sickness killing your sister's baby. She told me all about it.
About hospitals and ambulances and shots and oxygen and pills
and tests and I didn't understand none of it except them doctors
settled on a name and then quit. Said it might be weeks or
maybe a year but hardly more than that. Said they'd take the
baby and hook it up to machines but just a matter of time either
way so she kept the baby home. Kept her home and watched
her day and night and if somebody asked me I woulda said it's
the mama bout to die the way she looked when she come up
here with the baby on her back. Anybody be tired after climbing
Bruston Hill but there was something past tired in that girl's
face. Wasn't nothing to spare. Wasn't one patch of skin or
lump of fat or bone or muscle or gut string to spare. They was
all drawed out and all stretched thin as they could get and you
could see in her eyes, in the way she carried herself like she
weighed three hundred pounds when she wasn't nothing but
skin and bones, see how close she was to coming clean apart.
How easy it'd be for one string to snap and then all the rest
break down and she won't be nothing but jelly. And the baby
looked fine. Fuzzy little head running sweat under that cap but
she was a bouncy, smiley dimple-kneed sweet little brown baby
with the prettiest eyes in the world. Eyes that rolled and crossed
sometimes but you look at the two of them, look at mother and
daughter, and if you didn't know no better you be thinking the
poor babygirl gon be a orphan soon if her mama don't start
sleeping right or eating right or stop doing whatever it is make
her look like a ghost.

They thought I had a power so Shirl brought her baby to
see me and told me all about the terrible sickness and how it
was in those beautiful eyes already. How it would steal those
eyes and steal her ears and one day the lungs just forget all
about breathing and the heart forget about beating and it was
just a matter of time because those doctors named it and give
up. She said all that but never said nothing about me, about
that power supposed to be in somebody old and evil and crazy

because if you talk about it you can jinx it so you talk about everything else, talk around the power cause you don't want to jinx it. But I knew she ain't climbed Bruston Hill just to tell me her troubles so I listened and heard what she said and heard what she didn't say and thought about all the babies I kissed all the young ones pushed in my face and set on my lap. Wet ones and ones stink to high heaven and brown ones and black and white and fuzzy-headed and no hair at all and good hair like my side the family. Some of those children grown and down there in Homewood and God knows where else and some probably dead by now but they still coming with their babies so I sat there listening to your sister and tried to keep the power out my mind, tried not to jinx it or pray for it or promise it. Just sat there and tried to leave it be, tried to see the faces of the young ones I'd touched and tried to see them happy some-place and lucky someplace cause if they down there dying in the streets then why they keep coming to me? I tried to let the power be whatever it needed to be, tried to see that little girl running and grinning and rolling those big black eyes down there in Homewood with the rest of them.

When he come banging on my door I said Jesus I said Good God Almighty cause it don't matter what you are, don't matter if you a Christian or African, don't matter what you are as long as you got more sense than a stump you know there ain't nothing else to say when babies die and old dried-up just as soon dead as alive things like me left walking the earth. What kind of world is that? What kind of world give that baby beautiful eyes and then put in a drop of poison so they roll round like crazy marbles and she can't see nothing and can't hear and can't swallow her food? What kind of world is that? I'ma tell you what kind. It's the very kind run me up on this hill. It the kind won't leave you be no matter how far you run, no matter how much you hurry. It's the kind grab you and chew you up and spit you out and grind you into the dirt then grab you up again and start to chewing again just when you thought you wasn't nothing but dust and spit and wouldn't nothing touch you no more. That's the kind of world will catch you no matter how fast and how far you run. That's the kind of world always find something else to kill no matter how much you done buried already.

There wasn't nothing else to say. I just shuffled round here the rest of the day and tried to get used to those black eyes following me. And when they come on Wednesday I let them put me in a car and drive me down to Benson's and set me on a chair. That's the last time. Ain't nothing different down there. Never was. Never will be. Anybody got the sense they born with know what kind of world it is down there. But they still down there lying, still down there calling up *down*, and in *out*, and day *night*, and it don't make no difference. White or black or lying or telling the truth ain't nothing down there. Never was. Never will be. And if I had a mouth I'd tell em that when they come to carry me out the door. But you just a baby. You just sitting there because you ain't got no place else to go. You don't know what I'm talking about and no reason you should. You got young legs and young legs are for running, young legs will run cause that's their nature. They'll run till they get wore down to nubs then you still be trying to scoot around on the nubs cause that's the nature of young nubs and then you be in a chair when you ain't got nothing left below your hips to stand on and when you stuck in that chair you'll rock that chair and dream of running because that's the nature of old crippled-up fools. So ain't no need me trying to tell you nothing. And ain't no need of me listening to your troubles. And ain't no power ever gon change what's gon be. And what's gon be ain't never gon make no sense.

Look at you sitting there where she sat. Look at you wrapped in my blanket and your eyes don't even belong to you no more. Your eyes still down in them streets, your eyes still down there looking back over your shoulder to see who's after you. Scared rabbits in your eyes and why you got to be sitting there where she sat with that poor little pretty-eyed thing. I bet there was some of that pretty in your eyes once. I bet you had pretty long-lashed eyes when they still belonged to you.

So you mize well go on back to sleep. You been hit upside the head? Is that part of your troubles? Did somebody take a brick to your head cause I swear you got the sleeping sickness. You ain't done nothing but sleep since you been here. Standing up, lying down, sitting in a chair don't make no difference you sleeping. Outside, inside, hot or cold you sleeping. Who hit you upside your head, boy?

Talking all the time keep my ownself company and sure ain't gon stop now just cause you sitting here, so you can go to sleep or cut your eyes don't make me no nevermind. Do what I do all the time whether you here or not. Yes indeed.

Crazy as a bedbug but that don't make no nevermind neither cause I know all about you. Seen them rabbits in your eyes and gravedust on them long feet. Where else you gon be but out there in my shed?

CLEMENT

▼▼▼

Clement was trying to count the times. He needed to remember
the first time because you cannot begin without *one*, one was
first and he needed it to count the times he'd climbed Bruston
Hill for Miss Bess. The first time she wasn't Miss Bess. She
was the old woman one of the men said was kin. Old woman
lived alone on top of Bruston Hill and the man had dreamed
about her, dreamed two nights straight and Damnit I'm gon
play that dream I'm going to play it straight and combinade
it and box it and play it in all the houses in both races and get
out the Dream Book, Big Bob, git it out and read me that
number gon break the bank. The man said she was half-crazy,
an evil, funny-acting old woman who lived by herself like a
hermit up there but old folks in the family said she had power
said she had magic and he had dreamed about her two nights
and Git it out Big Bob, get out the Book and tell me the
numbers and find you a big box so you can put all my money
in when I breaks your bank.

Man said he was kin and said everybody in the family had
called her Mother Bess as long as he could remember so he
played it that way, Mother Bess, and played the dream lots of
other ways, bet all the money he could get his hands on but
spread it thin because he played the dream so many different
ways—Water and Fire and Death and Dreams and Old Woman
and Kin and Flying—but Mother Bess was how it hit. Straight
Mother Bess and he damned the other ways he tried to cover
the dream and damned the two nights of dreaming sent to
confuse him cause how a man gon to cover all the numbers in
two nights' worth of dreaming so he spread his money thin and
damned himself for not riding everything on *Mother Bess* because that's what it was about and she was magic and he just

should have stacked all the money on her. And damned his
luck quietly to himself but rode his luck like a fish-tailed, white
Eldorado through Big Bob's front door, riding it and shaking
Big Bob's door so it rang like a fire alarm. I told you. I told
you get a box. Didn't I tell that baggy-butt, no-hair-cutting
Negro to git hisself a box. Cause here I come and I want all
my money. Ring-a-ling-ling, I told you so. Now gimme my
money. Ring-a-ling-ling. Get your greasy yellow fingers in that
cash register and give it all to me.

Get away from that door, nigger. You letting in flies and
fools. Stop shaking that door fore you break something.

Already broke something. Broke your bank, Mr. Big Bob.

Shit. You ain't even scratched the behind of my bank. Now
get away from that door and get on over here so I can run my
hand down in my small change pocket and shut you up. Making
all that noise. Shit. Some niggers can't hold their drink. And
some can't hold their luck.

What you mumbling about? Your feelings hurt? Look at
him, you all. You ever seen a big fat yellow grown man so
close to crying?

You play, I pay. Ain't nothing to it. Just another day.

Ring-a-ling-ling-ling. Ring the bell for Mother Bess. Yes
indeed. The old folks know what they talking about. Gimme
my money so I can send something up the Hill. I'ma send her
a hundred dollar bill. Clement you know how to get up on
Bruston Hill. Soon's this colored gentleman pays me my money
I'ma send her a yard. You take it up and there's ten in it for
you cause I'm feeling good. Gon spread my luck around.

That was the first time. But it wasn't a hundred and it wasn't
ten. The man told him just keep walking and walking. If you
go past the old water tower up there you gone too far and walk
back a little ways you'll see where she lives over on the side.
Looks like there been a fire there or a wrecking ball but her
little shack's still standing in the middle of that mess. Ain't no
bigger than a chicken coop but that's it. Got a little raggedy
porch and she be sitting out there sometime. On your left as
you come up the hill. Just keep walking till there ain't no more
houses. Just about the top of the hill. Tall trees in the back.
Only house that high up the hill. Just keep on walking till you
think ain't no reason to keep walking and ain't nothing on this
damn hill but then you'll see it. If you come to the water tower
turn around. Come down a little bit you there.

Don't you lose this. This more money than you ever had
in your hand. So you better not lose it. And here's ten for you
cause I'm feeling good. Gon spread my luck around.

But the bill rolled and slipped in his fist was a ten. And the
bill rammed down in his pants pocket was a one. And the man
was scooting him out the door and winking because he knew
Clement could count. And the men always be lying. Lying
early in the morning. Lying till Big Bob shoos them out the
door and it rings the last time except once more when Big Bob
locks it and slams it behind him and Clement is alone and the
lies still crawling cross the floor, sticking in his broom, hiding
under the dirt balls and hair balls so he can still hear those lies
as he sweeps the floor, hear them plain as he hears the door
saying good-bye when it says hello, as he hears it saying Big
Bob is gone again and it's night and saying Big Bob is here
again and it's morning.

The first time. The *one* he needs to begin, so he counts it,
counts the long hike up and up till ain't no more houses and
ain't no more sidewalk. Then he finds it and the porch bends
like it might try to eat him and he knocks one, two, three times.
Hard but not hard enough to cave in the wall ain't none too
solid so he is looking back over his shoulder deciding which
way he'll run if the skimpy house starts to falling, checking
over his shoulder all the way back down the hill to Big Bob's
when she says, What you pounding on my door for? Don't you
ever pound on my door like that again. What you want, boy?

Her face is made from the boards of the shack. She is
browner and they are more grey but you could patch a hole in
the weathered wooden walls with her face and never know the
difference. Same lines and cracks and if you ran your finger
cross it same splinters stick you. He almost asks, Is you a
witch, lady? Almost tells her the story of Hansel and Gretel
so she'll know he knows about that oven she got inside and
the sharp knives and he ain't about to bend over so she can
push him in.

You got a mouth?

He sees hers. Sees a moustache like a man's and her bottom
lip got those spidery cracks like the boards.

He sent me give you this.

Sees her little eyes buried in the creases and the more you
look the more you see the green staring back at you and the
green is not the color of her eyes it is something in her eyes,

specks of something in there that came before the eyes got buried in her face. The green flecks heavy as chips of stone and that's why her eyes are so heavy, are sinking, that's why they stare through you from deep back where they are sinking in her head.

Who sent who to gimme what?

He said he played Mother Bess and Big Bob had to pay him so he stopped messing with the door and told me take this up Bruston Hill. It's money and he gave me a tip. He lied but they always be lying. It's ten and I got one.

Half them fools down there be calling me Mother Bess and I ain't mama to none them. Never been mama to nobody but once and that's all over, that's so long ago it don't make no nevermind. If one them fools fool enough give away they money I'll take it. Serve him right talking that Mother Bess mess and I sure ain't his mama whoever it is. Who is you, boy?

Clement.

You Clement, is you? Ain't never knowed a Clement. Didn't know there was a Clement in Homewood but they got all kinds of funny names down there now. Like those names make a difference. Like they somebody else just cause they got one them funny names. Changing names and taking names ain't never changed no niggers in Homewood. Well, you tell him I didn't say thanks. You tell him, Mr. Clement, I didn't say nothing and I sure ain't his mama. And glad of it. You tell him that for me, boy. You got any name side Clement?

No, Mam.

Well somebody taught you a little manners even if they ain't taught you no name.

Miss Claudine.

What you say?

Supposed to put Good morning fore your Gimmes.

I guess if you had sense enough to get up here from Homewood and hand me this money you got sense enough to get back down again even if you don't make sense while you up here. You take this back to Big Bob. He the one writing numbers ain't he? He still run numbers out his barbership ain't he? No reason for him not to less he's dead. Unless somebody shot him for messing with they money. You said something about Big Bob's so you know what I'm talking about. He been running numbers out there since before I come up on this hill. You know what I'm talking about, don't you?

Yes, Mam.

Well carry this money back down there and you tell him put it all on seven-fifty-three. You hear that? Seven-fifty-three on the first race. The whole ten right on that. And tell him put my money in this bag.

Yes, Mam. Seven-fifty-three.

And you know why it's gon be seven-fifty-three? Course you don't, but I'ma tell you when you bring my money up here tomorrow. Now you hurry and do what I told you. Ain't got all day to get a number in. Not unless they changed it. And ain't no reason to change it. Ain't no reason to change nothing cause it don't make no difference. But you gon and do what I told you. Seven-fifty-three on the first race. You come back tomorrow with my money in that bag and I'll tell you why it got to be seven-fifty-three.

That was *one* so he is beginning to count. Two was what came next, came when Big Bob shooed them out that night and locked the door and turned out all the lights but one and filled the paper sack with money. The bell said what it been saying all day and Big Bob said: I ain't messing with no Hoodoo Woman. I ain't taking no more her numbers. She got this but that's all. Sending a child down here with one number like that and it hit straight on the nose. It ain't natural. It ain't legal. This is Big Bob talking. This is Big Bob and I pays when you plays but I ain't messing with no two-headed witch sends numbers by children and sends paper bags to put her money in.

Big Bob walking cross the floor and getting in his medicine. But it ain't in no cup of warm milk from Miss Claudine or nothing just the long-necked bottle of J&B and he swallows hard and almost chokes hisself. His fingers go behind the barber coat but he can't get it right the first time. They miss. They don't have eyes tonight because they miss the first time and Big Bob walks the floor end to end, from the window to the back and one more time then he finds the string and unwraps his barber coat and looks at hisself in all the mirrors. Back front and sides all at once if you stand the right way and know how to look because that's how you got to do when you cutting hair. You got to see front and back and sides to get it even. He stands beside the chair looking the way he does when somebody's in it and he don't feel like cutting hair. Just looking like he trying to figure something real special to do with that head in the chair, but he just cut one head too many and he's looking cause he's tired, looking cause he's bone tired and he can't think of nothing better to do than look.

That's right. Can't be no other way. Ain't supposed to be no other way. Can't fight no Hoodoo Lady.

Like he didn't know till just that night and just that bagful of money that he been carrying all that Big Bob weight. Like he knows all the sudden he's been carrying all that yellow meat and ain't had time to be tired till just that night and now he got to be tired this one night for all those other days and nights and he carries that Big Bob weight twice up and back the floor from the back to the red sign twice, and can't do it no more, might not do it never no more. Don't even slam the door, just prise it open easy and turns the key and slides it so it hardly rings, so it just says good-bye and nothing else.

Seven-fifty-three. Ain't nothing special about it. It just come to me is all. I seen it plain as I used to see them letters writ up in the sky. Airplane make a sign up there and you could read it all over Homewood. Saw that number plain as day and knew it was the one and that's why I give you that sack and that's why I'm sitting here this early in the morning waiting for my money.

(Two). He can't sleep. He keeps the bag on his mattress under the blanket with him and the bag rattles and squirms and talks to him all night. So he's up before dawn and hauling butt up Bruston Hill and doesn't even see the sun rise over the city and burnish the hills so all of Pittsburgh is a flaming sea of lava sliding down from Bruston Hill into the rivers he couldn't see even if he was paying attention to anything beside the brown paper sack full of money in his fist. She had promised to tell him her secret and that was on his mind but they said curiosity kilt the cat so it wasn't just curiosity caught him by the scruff of his neck and jerked him up the hill before dawn. He was up and setting down one foot after the other in the blue streets because she called him, because her voice was there in Big Bob's backroom and it wasn't a question of saying yes or no to her but seeing how fast he could get up there with her money. But not so much a voice as a whistle. And not so much the money as it was a matter of returning her bag.

(Two). Is hurrying and out of breath and a moment when

the porch is like a grey whale stretching its jaws open and just might swallow him if she doesn't answer the tapping of his fingers on the hangnail door.

How somebody supposed to hear you scratching like that? Mize well knock with a feather. Jump up here and just about kick a hole in my porch then you scratching with a feather like nobody ain't heard you just about knock my house down jumping up here.

You set that down on the table. Young boy like you oughtn't have too much cash money. Just get you in trouble. I'ma give you this dollar and give you more a little bit at a time but give it steady so you always got a little something in your pocket but not enough get you in trouble. You take this and they'll always be some more you come round and run to the store for me and do a few little chores need done round here you always gon have a piece of money in your pocket. You understand me? You understand what I'm talking about, boy?

Yes, Mam.

And that seven-fifty-three. Just forget about that seven-fifty-three. Just got lucky is all. Seven-five-three. Ain't nothing special about it. It just come to me is all. Seen it plain as I used to see them wooly white letters writ up in the sky. Airplane make a sign up there and you could read it all over Homewood. I saw that number plain as day and knew it was the one and that's why I give you that sack and that's why I'm sitting here this early in the morning waiting for my money.

That ain't all there is to it. Course not. But you too young to understand the rest. I could tell you but it's too deep. It's the number my man wore on a chain round his neck. Little round piece of metal, the color of a penny and like a penny somebody had stomped down and mashed thin. Wasn't like nothing I seen before. Didn't have nothing on it but that number 753. Don't know where he got it. I asked him and he said it's my luck. A kinda long silvery kind of chain around his neck and he never took it off and that dog tag always dangling at the end. Never said nothing but it's my luck. I called it a dog tag and he grinned when I said that. I liked to play with it. Shut my eyes and feel the number with the tip of my fingers. Swing it and dangle it and finger it where it was warm from laying against his chest. But you don't know nothing about nothing like that. Never thought there'd be a day I could slip it off over his head and he wouldn't say stop or wouldn't grab

my hand. Never thought there'd be a day I could just take it
and have it if I wanted it. Never thought I'd leave it laying
there on his chest and say good-bye to it and not have it to turn
in my fingers and slide up and down that silvery chain while
I teased him and called it a dog tag to make him grin. But it's
long gone and he's long gone so all that don't make no nevermind. All it makes is seven five three floating before my
eyes like those smoky white letters Atlantic and Pacific in the
sky. And makes a bag of dollars. And makes seven days and
seven sins and seven come eleven if you shooting crap. And
five got that hook. Five is a fisher. Five is fever. Five is staying
alive. You leave out the evens. You give the white folks the
evens. They likes things neat. Two-four-six-eight-ten. Two by
fours and ten little Indins all in a row. They like things with
corners, things you can break in half, things that got a nature
you can tame. But what you gon do with the odds? That's why
they's the odds. You got your nine at one end and your one
on the other. Now what you gon do with that? Seven-five-
three. That's the middle, that's the heart of the odds. Three
right next to the gate but it got to wait. Can't get over. Can't
get under. Can't get around. But three's trying. Circling ev-
erywhich way. Got curves and straight and zigzags. Got a hook
too like five. But three is at the gate. Three is two faces and
two eyes can't see each other but sees everything else. Three
got a mirror in its belly. But how you gon know what I'm
talking about. You just a baby. Ain't no way you can get as
deep as I'm going and I ain't even wet yet. I'm just playing
numberology and trickology. Ain't nothing to it anyway. Just
got lucky with 753.

So Clement had *one* and had *two* and the rest be easy. He'd
hear her whistle stomp through the streets of Homewood. Hear
her walking stick tap, tap, tap and she be standing over him
crooking her finger and, Come on boy, hurry up boy her face
like somebody took one of those boards off the raggedy shack
and poked eye holes, poked nose holes and dug out a mouth.
A kind of whistle, howl, moaning call nobody could hear but
him when it reached down off Bruston Hill and started to lift
houses and pull up sidewalks and tear blue shadows apart to
find him.

But now he'd have to start his count again because now it
wasn't going up the hill to do for her but going up the hill to
do for *them*. That ghost he had only heard the first time it was

up there. That ghost who was the one all the men were talking about. He had never heard her say the ghost's name but Clement knew it was him, was that Tommy Lawson they said killed a man and robbed that dago Indovina the fence. Killed Chubby they said. Said it was a miracle Chubby ain't been dead nine or ten times before. Said his luck finally run out. This time somebody blowed that fool's head off sure enough. Chubby been going for bad since he was old enough to spit. Chubby just as soon walk through people as walk around em. Chubby got hands like a gorilla. A crying shame God put such a little bitty brain in all that body. Yeah, he liked to walk around with his shirt off in the summer showing his muscles. Well, he had some muscles to show. He was big alright. And they say he knew all that Hi Karate and Jew jitsu and stuff. Big as he was wasn't nobody gon mess with him don't care what somebody knew or didn't know. Big burly nigger walking round with his shirt off like Tarzan in the grocery store and who gon tell that big sucker to put it back on. Walked the streets like he owned them. Said he killed a man in prison. Beat him to death with his hands. Prison ain't nothing but a jungle. That ain't all he killed. You remember that mess about Valdez in the paper. All them killings on the North side and those massage parlors and that mess. Well Chubby was in that too. They caught Valdez but Chubby was in it too. Makes sense. He was always hanging with Valdez. And both of them mean niggers Tomming for the dagos. It was just a matter of time. Somebody bound to blow his head off sooner or later. Ain't nothing but a cat got nine lives and you look round here you see plenty dead cats. Yeah, don't care how many lives you got one day they run out, one day you dead don't care how lucky you are, don't care how many dagos covering your ass.

Clement listened. Down in the Homewood streets. Up on Bruston Hill. The man staying with Mother Bess wasn't no ghost, he was a natural man who ate beans and chewed apples and drank Henry Bow's moonshine.

Mother Bess said, You don't see nothing. You understand? You don't see nothing, nor hear nothing and you sure ain't gon say nothing, you understand?

Yes, Mam.

This boy gon be here awhile but you don't see nothing. He's sitting at that table big as life but you don't see him do you?

No, Mam.

That's good. That's nice. Clement a good boy. You don't have to worry none bout Clement. And Clement ain't got nothing to worry about cause ain't nothing here for him to worry about.

Yes, Mam . . . No, Mam.

The man she called a boy. The man Clement could see through but who wasn't no ghost, that Tommy Lawson they all talking bout in Big Bob's and Miss Claudine's and the Brass Rail. He the one Carl and that stranger talking about and he ain't caught yet. Him nor his partner Ruchell. Tommy Lawson's the one. Still loose. But he ain't a thousand miles away. Just up on Bruston Hill in her house.

Or in her backyard like he saw him the third day. The first time was inside, was morning and Clement could hear her talking to somebody before he even got to the porch. He remembered the ghost trying to sneak out the back door. The ghost shouting at him through the wooden walls, *I ain't here, Goddamnit. Go away. I ain't here.* How his ears hurt and head hurt and how he froze on the porch and couldn't take a step forward or couldn't take one backward because the ghost voice inside the shack was warning him, was threatening him, was screaming *I ain't here, Goddamnit* in the silence so the silence was thick as weeds and the screaming was a snake in the weeds and if he put his foot down on the noisy boards the snake would strike. But he had called her and knocked anyway, knocked not for her to answer but to let the ghost know he was there and let the ghost know he wasn't sneaking around but getting out of there as fast as his feet could get him down off the porch. She answered the knock and chased him away and he hadn't seen nothing, just felt the whole house shake when the ghost sneaked out the back. He hadn't seen nothing the first time and the second time neither. Because she told him look through the man, past the man who wasn't a ghost but flesh and blood like her, like him. A natural man with a natural name. Tommy Lawson. But she said you ain't seen nothing so that's what he saw when he brought the shopping bag of groceries the afternoon of the second day. Nothing at the table drinking a cup of something.

The third day he saw nothing in the backyard, nothing on its hands and knees digging in the dirt. A narrow-butt nothing with holes in the bottom of its high-heeled shoes. Digging and straightening up sticks and pushing sticks in. A pile of weeds raked off to one side. Tools scattered around the patch of dug-up earth. Clement had followed Mother Bess through the house. If you counted her legs you'd get three most of the time. And when she poked that bowed walking stick out to the front and side of her the way she does she is as wide as she is high, she makes a circle with that stick in her hand. So he follows the grey sweater which is loose and raggedy and droops like a dusty spider web from her shoulders in the middle of the circle, follows it through the house and doesn't look right or left but keeps his eyes on the bullseye, a rubbed bare spot where there's a lump between her shoulder blades. Because it's easier that way to see nothing and nothing might not even see you if you mind your own business so he follows her through the house and out the back door and it's daylight again, the sun slaps him across the face and for a moment till he blinks away the sharp light he sees nothing till he sees nothing's scrawny backside.

You want this boy bring you something?

Got no money.

You want this boy bring you something, I said?

Iron City. A case. Yeah. And each one sweatin cold. Sure, you tell him a case of cold Iron City.

Get a quart long with the other things.

I'm bout to die out here in all this sun. Ain't no goddamn farmer. Ain't used to scrabbling around in the dirt on my hands and knees.

He is standing. He is like the tall trees don't start to filling out with branches and leaves till near the top. Lean and straight till the wild burst of his Afro.

That's enough cutting and digging. I'm sweating like a pig. Hot and thirsty as I am even that castor oil you got running in your pipes gon taste good. All I wanted was to plant me a seed or two. Didn't know about all the rest of this mess.

If you gon sow you got to prepare the ground. And preparing means chopping weeds and turning the soil.

You sure these seeds still good. How long they been sitting here?

What you mean good?

Alive. They still alive? The way they rattle inside here sounds like they long gone.

Course they dead. Supposed to be dead. Why else you think you bury em in the ground? They dead and you put em

in the ground so they can die some more, so they can split open
and come apart and get mixed up with what's in the soil and
go to growing again. You citified children don't know nothing.
Growing up where ain't nothing but pavement youall probably
think you plant a hambone to grow a pig.

I ain't never planted nothing in my life. Grew up thinking
everything came from stores. You right about that. Everything
came from the white man on the corner or from the A&P up
on Homewood Avenue. I ain't never tried to grow nothing.

If you gon try this time you get them packets of seeds off
the table and come on back outside. It's already late in the
season. Just might be too late to get some of them seeds to
grow but you bring em all. You ain't too old to learn. Get you
a cup of water and come on so I can show you what to do.
You gon learn to do it right.

Her hair is grey. But grey is not one thing, it's all the colors
from white to black, twisted, tangled under the net sits like a
bag atop her head. Ain't curly like a nigger's hair. Long fine
threads hang out the bottom of the net. The back of her neck
is browner than the boards but deep-grained like the boards,
creases long and fine as the wisps of hair hanging out the bag.

You still here, boy? What you staring at with your pop-eyed
self?

No, Mam.

A quart of beer with the rest.

Can he get a bag of ice someplace?

He ain't no mule.

Where's the jug. Can't drink this nasty water without nothing in it. It'd be better cold than warm. Little ice might help.

Clement hears but he is not listening. The door closes behind
him and his feet sink and he's going down the hill for *them*,
not for her, so he'll have to start all over again. Start with *one*
again.

TOMMY

▼▼▼▼▼▼▼▼▼▼▼▼▼▼▼▼▼▼▼▼▼▼▼▼▼▼▼▼▼▼▼▼▼▼▼▼▼

He says, *Well, that's that, old woman,* not knowing exactly
what he means, saying the words because he's heard them
before and said them before so they come easy but he doesn't
know what he means, hadn't planned to say anything until the
words come out just as he said them, almost as if they had
found him and used him to say something they needed to say,
used him and didn't bother to let him know what they were
talking about. *Well, that's that.* And he addressed the words
to her because she was in the dark room with him, because she
had taught him to plant, because she sent the boy for Iron City,
because she was sipping nasty shine in nasty water with him
and it had been three days now and he was tired now, and high
enough now to need somebody else to speak to, to draw him
out of the fog into which he was sinking. The fog of his own
thoughts, his own body, his own life which was settling over
him again like the darkness draping her shack.

I got to leave here.

Then he knew what the other words were talking about,
why they had found him and used his mouth.

Are you listening to me, old woman? How you think you
know so much bout people's business and you always talking
never give nobody a chance to open his mouth? You still ain't
heard me.

When I was your age all I did was listen. When I was your
age in a room with the old people I kept my mouth shut cause
I believed there might be someoody know'd more than me and
if I kept my mouth shut I might learn something.

That ain't what I'm talking about. That ain't got nothing
to do with it.

I'm tired, boy. You done disturbed me out my usual ways
and I'm wore out and my head feels like it's full of broken

glass and I don't want nothing rattling round in there so you speak soft or don't say nothing but don't you raise your voice one iota.

It's been three days now and I think I better go on back down there and do what I have to do.

They be waiting. They got plenty time. You be dead and buried ten times over they still got plenty time. They the patientest things in the world.

I ain't worried bout the cops no more.

That ain't all that's down there means you harm.

Well, I ain't worried bout nothing no more.

Fast work is all I can say. Mighty fast work. It ain't hardly been three days you crawled up here like something the cat drug in and now you fixing to walk out like King Kong ain't afraid of nothing. Mighty fast.

Wouldna been three days. Wouldna been five minutes if I left when you told me to leave. Sleeping in some damn shed. Come damn near freezing to death. You supposed to be kin. You supposed to be my people and you run me off like I was a disease. So don't be talking bout *how long*. According to you just knocking at your door was too long. Had to shove that wood around and crawl inside there and sleep on the ground like some wild animal.

Where else you gon stay? Course you slept out there. If you had someplace else to go you sure would have gone and I'da been happy to see you go. Happy as a tick on a bloody bedbug. I knew you was out there. I came and got you, didn't I?

After I froze my butt off.

Wrapped you in a blanket off my own bed. Fed you. Listened to your nasty mouth.

Don't start on nasty mouths now, old woman. Ain't never heard nobody talk mean and evil till I heard you. And you don't even cuss. Cussing ain't cold enough for you. No wonder you ain't got no refrigerator up here. Hot as it's been you don't miss ice. You got that cold blood, that ice water blood. Talking bout I was born to die. Telling me I got to pay the piper and it ain't none your business some cop blow me away.

Nothing cold bout the truth. It's just the truth. Like they say the truth and nothing but the truth and that's what makes it true.

How come you ain't got nothing up here? No TV or radio or nothing? Like living in a cave. Gets dark outside and it's dark in here. I'm gon send you a radio up here. A nice transistor runs by battery. Least you could have some music up here.

Don't need that mess. Got my oil lamp. Got candles. Got all I need. And where you gon get money for some radio, anyway? You the one crying since you been here cause you ain't got a dime in your pocket.

I know how to get things.

Bet you do. I bet you a real outlaw.

Do what I have to do to get by.

And what's that? Robbing folks and messing with that dope and killing people so people trying to kill you. What kind of life is that?

My life. The only one I've had.

Didn't have to be that way. Everybody down there ain't like that. You got a brother done alright for hisself. He's a snotty, dicty-talking nigger but he made something of hisself. Plenty people down there ain't got squat but they ain't stealing and robbing. They ain't outlaws.

Tell me bout it. Tell me about Mr. Barclay work all his life and got a raggedy truck and a piece of house and they call him Deacon in the church and when he dies ain't gon have the money for a new suit to be buried in. Tell me about the plenty. Old people burning up in shacks. Kids ain't even ten years old and puffing weed and into anything they can get their hands on. Tell me about those fools marching off to Nam and coming back cripples and junkies and strungout worse than these niggers in the street. And coming back dead. Plenty. Yeah you tell me bout plenty and I'll tell you bout jail and tell you bout old home week because that's where everybody at. It's like high school reunion in there, everybody I grew up with's in there or on the way or just getting back. I got your plenty. Shit. Plenty fools just sitting there letting all the shit fall on their heads ain't got the sense to move. I tried. I could tell you something bout trying. Oh yeah. Work and raise a family they say. Then they say sorry ain't no work. Then ain't no family. Then they say you ain't shit. Then you do what you have to do and you really ain't shit. You an outlaw. But that's what you supposed to be in the first place. And that's my life. The only one I've had. And they gon take that if they can.

Damn. I wish you had some music in here, old woman. It's too damn quiet in here.

Ain't no dance hall.

You got that right.

People used to make they own music. Could play and sing and make music all night long.

Bet you did. Banjos and guitars and harps and all that ole time jumping around and down home hollering.

Best music ever was. Kind of music you can't hear on no radio. You got to be there, you got to be making it or dancing to it or singing with the one singing.

Did you dance, old woman? Did you strut your stuff and shimmy wobble shake? Bet you did. Bet you was cold and mean too. Bet you was a fox in your day, Old Bess. Breaking hearts and carrying on.

Watch your mouth.

Why you stay up here, old woman? You scared ain't you? You been just as scared up here as I been down there. And if I'm hiding, you're hiding too. But I'm hiding so I can run. You just hiding. You let them whip all the run out you. I don't want to go that way.

Had a man who could whistle more music than you find in all them radios. You don't know nothing about the blues. Youall missed the blues.

Thought you was cool at first. Evil and mean and half crazy but cool. You know what I mean. Like nothing could touch you. Like you in your own bag, like you had your shit so together you didn't need nothing or nobody and I felt like a damn fool begging to stay in your house. So cool. Cold cool and even though I thought about busting your head and staying here anyway I was digging you. Digging that cool. Cause that's me. I been trying to stay cool all my life. That's the game. That's what you learn. You got to be cool to stay alive. But what the fuck has cool got me? I been cool and look at me. Stuck in some damn slave cabin.

Youall ain't never heard no music. Hmmmmp.

Hey now. If you gon pour, do me too. Mize well get good and fucked up before I leave here. Mize well go on and get my head real bad before I fight them streets. Because I'm leaving. That's that. I can't stay up here no longer. Got to be more to it than staying cool. Maybe when you get old it's easy. Maybe you got yourself together and nothing don't matter no more. Maybe you'll just keep on hiding up here till one day that boy, Clement, finds you dead. Like you always be telling me, that's your business. But it ain't no life. That ain't no life for me I got to take a chance. As messed up as I am I got to get down from here and take my chance.

He could whistle a different blues every time. Just make it up as he goes along and that music be steady talking to you. You'd hear its name and it'd be talking to you plain as day. Different every time but the same too. You'd know the name, you'd hear the name plain as day and think, Hello, hello Mister Hair Brushing Blues. What you got to say today?

I been scared all my life. But I ain't scared now. I ain't killed nobody. Didn't even see Ruchell waste Chubby. They can't put that on me. They can kill me but I still ain't killed nobody and I ain't scared. All they can do is kill me cause I ain't going back to nobody's goddamn jail.

I was scared a long time. Ever since my granddaddy John French died and his house fell to pieces and everybody scattered I been scared. Scared of people, scared of myself. Of how I look and how I talk, of the nigger in me. Scared of what people said about me. But I got no time to be scared now. Ain't no reason to be scared now cause ain't nothing they can take from me now. Lost my woman, lost my son, shamed all the family I got down there. So it's just me and I know I ain't killed nobody so fuck em. Motherfuck em I say. Let them find me and kill me if they can but I know who I am and know what I did, and I'm ready to live now. I ain't ready to die. Hell no. I'm ready to live and do the best I can cause I ain't scared.

That's moonshine talking now. Henry Bow got your tongue and turning it every whichway but loose. Talking like you down there in one of them saloons.

Yeah. You Hard Hearted Hannah, alright. You mize well be under this goddamn hill. You mize well be sitting inside it, riding it like a tank. Ain't nothing gon touch you till that Clement breaks in here and puts his hand on your forehead. And that boy think he's touching ice. And that ice gon burn his young fingers.

I ain't the one running down to Homewood putting my brain up against some policeman's pistol. I ain't the one can't wait to get back down there in them streets where people hunting for me. You go back down there and I'll be hearing about you. It'll be Clement alright, but Clement come to tell me you sure nuff ain't scared of nothing no more.

Tell me bout it. Tell me bout hunting wild animals. Tell me bout dogs in alleys waking up the neighborhood. Tell me bout flashlights poking in the shadow where you trying to cop a minute's sleep. Don't you think I know bout that? Don't you think I want it different? Don't you think I tried?

It's your business.

It's my business. It's the only goddamn business I'm gon to get.

Tonight.

This very goddamn dreary quiet ain't got no choice night, old woman. Old Mother Bess. Finish this cup of moonshine and put my foot in the path and say good-bye. Say thank you Mother Bess even if you don't want to hear all that mess, even if you cuss me with your fine old cold self.

BESS

▼▼

Is it a month, a year, a week, is it the very night he left? She can't tell, can't tell if she's dreaming or if he's been long gone or just tripped out the back door five minutes before. First there had been the stomping and pounding loud as thunder, loud enough to raise the dead because that's what she was, dead in a Henry Bow moonshine sleep and it would take thunder or an atom bomb to jerk her back to life. She knows it's too soon to be awake. She knows she was just starting that good deep sleep. Then the pounding and stomping. She groaned out loud and knew sleep was gone, knew the dreaming which hadn't begun yet would never start. She was reaching for the stick at the head of the bed. Her clothes were still on. Tangled, sticking to her like what was left of sleep. She couldn't see the hand she held in front of her face, the hand batting at the net teasing her eyes. Sitting up in bed she coughed and felt the top of her head fly off. The room was spinning or she was spinning or she sat headless, mired in her twisted clothes while the ball that had once rested on her neck whirled round the room like a runaway top. She was an old woman startled awake in the middle of the night. Like somebody was snapping on lights, powerful, piercing lights that smoked and seared and popped and blinded. From a stupor to this sudden hurting light. She let the stick clatter to the floor. Rubbed both fists in her eyepits to restore the darkness.

Somebody had stomped across her porch. Somebody had pounded on her door. It had to be him. Couldn't be nobody but him. Running. He would be in the shed again. His long feet stomping across her porch and now they'd be poked out the end of the wood shed because he was a tall lean thing like those trees and it hurt her to see those feet when they were so still, so long and raggedy because she could see the run in

153

them, the scared rabbit eyes in them as plain as the holes in his high-heeled shoes.

He was Lizabeth's son and Lizabeth was Freeda's girl. The quiet one born too soon in a snowstorm and May grabbed up the blue baby and plunged it in a snowdrift and the open door crashed again and again like a broken wing against the frame. Her man getting drunk on Dago Red with John French and singing all night long after Freeda's first child was born dead and saved. John French would carry his little girl on his shoulders to Bruston Hill and Lizabeth would ride down on the sled her man made. Her man was good with his hands. He could make anything he wanted to make. She watched her man's brown hand play up and down her naked thigh, she saw it sanding the boards smooth and shiny, saw it paint-flecked as the brush turned the boards of little Lizabeth's sled bright red. His hand patting the head of the child she couldn't give him, his voice, hold on little motorcar driver, hold on little sky flyer, just hold on and steer with your feet and your Daddy John be there at the bottom to catch you. And after all those years of waiting Eugene finally growing inside her belly and her man's hand plays up and down her plump thigh, her swollen belly and he's saying Hold on, hold on little sweet thing and snow is falling around her and she can barely stand up on the slick cobbled street but she makes the trip every day rain shine snow don't make no nevermind because it's not a letter she hopes to find at the bottom of Bruston Hill. No, because letters lie and nobody but a fool believes what letters say nobody but a fool would be outside in all this snow, fighting all this ice just to get a letter. No, it would be her son Eugene she'd find, find him one bright morning rain shine or snow didn't make no nevermind he'd be there and catch her in his young strong arms when she flew the last few steps off the hill.

He was Lizabeth's son and his sister had brought the pretty-eyed baby for Mother Bess to touch, to lay on her crippled hands and blow her stale Henry Bow breath on the brown baby cheeks. Lady bug, Lady bug fly away. To be magic, to sing magic, to touch with the power they believed she had because she was old and evil and crazy up there by herself on top of Bruston Hill. Because she lived with the dead. Because she was dead herself.

It had to be him, but was it yesterday, last week, just a moment ago that he had stomped through her black, dreamless sleep and cracked all the boards of her door and ripped the covers off her bed so she bolted up shivering and afraid and dreaming.

Where had he learned that song? She was outside and he was in the house, still wrapped in the blanket and she thought still sleeping but people didn't whistle while they were asleep so when she had heard the song she knew he was awake or knew her man was inside with him because what she heard was blues like her man whistled. For the first time in thirty some years she had pulled herself up from the rocker and stepped toward the music and it hadn't stopped. Hadn't faded or run from her so she took another step across the noisy boards and the whistled blues still didn't run, still didn't hide till she pushed through the door and stared at the boy wrapped up like an Indin at her table. The blues hadn't stopped till he said, I thought you was sleep out there and she said, I thought you was sleep in here.

But that last night, that night a year ago or hours ago or whenever it was if it ever was, she had said, Youall don't know nothing bout no blues. Wasn't that what she had told him? Wasn't that the way it had to be? Because once was enough. Once was one time too many to watch people sing the blues and die. Once was enough to listen and then have it all go away and have nothing but silence. Once and then you got to say good-bye say yes I'm hiding, yes I'm scared but what you know about it? How you gon know anything about it? It ain't none your business. Ain't nobody's business.

She hears a car racing up the hill. It is rushing all the way to the top dragging tin cans and garbage cans behind it, losing its wheels, its doors, pounded apart the way Bruston Hill always pounds apart any car tries to climb its steep, broken side too fast. The darkness winks at her. Opens and shuts its eye so the walls flicker like they're on fire. No one drives up Bruston Hill at night. No one runs across her porch and beats on her door. She had said good-bye. She had said no more of that mess. But the darkness winks and she can see cold light buckling the walls, light flashing in the corners, light touching her things.

It had to be him. And it had to be them after him. She scoots her hips faster than she thought she could to the edge of the bed. Her stocking feet tap the bare floor once but the second time they're on target and she wiggles her toes into the mashed back slippers. She stoops for the cane and realizes how

fast she's moving when her back says No says I still got the
weight of the world on these old shoulders and you better
straighten up slow, real slow if you want to straighten up at
all.

Old as she is she has good ears. She hears what she wants
to hear. The stick picking its way across the room to the front
door, the stick tapping the swaybacked boards. It's him. Who
else it gon be? And she hears him telling his troubles and hears
herself shushing him and hears him snoring and laughing and
whistling and telling lies and damning her and something crack-
ing, like ice, like a brittle shell. Almost on the beat. Less a
crackling than quick loud pops following one another like fire-
works on the Fourth of July. Her fist is wrapped around the
knobby head of the stick. She crashes it against the porch
boards, almost on the beat, echoing the string of gunshots
exploding in the darkness. She squeezes so hard she can feel
the stick coming through the back of her hand, feels it cutting
and pushing deeper every time she raises it, everytime she digs
it into the splitting wood.

Oh Jesus. Oh God.

How you know so much about people you never give them
a chance to open they mouth? How you know so much?

She cannot turn it loose. Her crippled fingers are knotted
over the top of the stick. Her arm trembles and the crooked
stick trembles with it as she tries to steady herself, as she needs
all three legs to hold herself up.

Oh Jesus. Oh Good God Almighty.

She damns the weakness that makes her stand there shaking.
She damns the crackle of gunfire and damns the sudden stillness
that has followed the shots, a stillness broken only by the
sweeping light which makes the crest of the hill blink off and
on like a red neon sign.

Only two shuffled steps to the rocker. Against the night
chill, against the dew wetting her bare skin when it touches
the arm of the chair, she pulls the grey sweater tighter round
her shoulders. Slumped in the chair she feels the blood returning
to her hand; her fingers unclench, the stick clatters again to the
floor of the porch. A circle of pain in the palm of her hand,
a hot, stinging trace of the gnarled stick's head away from
which her stiff fingers slowly uncurl.

She can hear sirens whining down below in the city. Above
her in the darkness she has turned away from, a voice broadcasts

over a radio, a voice frying in bursts of static, a voice she damns and tries to drown in the squeak and groan of the rocker.

More sirens climb the hill. People used to tie cans and stuff to the Just Married cars. Cans and the crepe paper so the cars rattled and fluttered through the Homewood streets. You'd hear them most on a Saturday morning. That crash and rattle and some fool always leaning on his horn and the train of three or four fancied-up cars would rule the streets till they went on about their business and you'd wonder who it was, wonder if you knew them after you couldn't hear them no more. So the heavy-footed police cars rumbled up the hill, screaming to the top like something terrible was chasing them. And the crest of the hill ablaze now with spinning red lights. One long finger of light traces the shape of the tower, finds the curving ladder and follows it to the top, pausing, pointing for a moment where the ladder touches the lip of the huge pot atop the steel legs. She gets up from her chair and steps off the porch long enough to see the false red dawn and the pointing white spotlight, long enough to know she is too old and frail to go any farther. Too weak to punish the police swarming over Bruston Hill just beyond her view. She damns them and hobbles back to her porch, an old woman startled from her sleep in the middle of the night, an old woman in a dark house who knows it's too late to help him, who knows he's long gone, who knows her arms are too weak to lift him and carry him back where he belongs.

She damns her weakness. She strikes a match and lights the grocery bags she had balled up and stuffed under the grate of the stove. Her shadow dances across the ceiling and walls. In the far corner of the room she thinks she sees a spark rising, a bluish spark cast off by the fire in the stove. But it doesn't die as it floats towards the ceiling. The blue spark wheels and climbs and soars and then she realizes it is the angel in the blue-eyed gown, the angel who took apart the cobweb strand by strand and moved it and put it back together again so it could catch the colored light streaming through the stained glass window in Benson's. Her patient little blue-gowned angel who wouldn't hurt a soul, who wouldn't hurt anything. The spark was the flame-tipped wand in her tiny angel hand. She flits through the darkness like a lightning bug, touching this and that with her wand. What she kisses bursts into flame. She has beautiful black eyes. She darts and swoops and zigzags and leaves a trail of blossoming flames. The angel in the blue-eyed gown works with her to set the house on fire.

We gon do it, gal. Yes we are. Thank you you little blue-gowned, black-eyed thing. Thank you you little fuzzy-headed got the prettiest black-eyed lazy Susan eyes in the whole world thing. Don't matter if they's crossed a little bit, don't matter if they roll round sometime like they ain't got no strings and gon on about they own business. And you. You get up off that bed, man. Cause it's going too, everything in here going so get your whistling self up off that bed and come on.

He still has sleep in his eyes. Her man's still drowsy and she has to push him out the door. The angel is long gone, gone the same way she got in. Angels have power. Angels will always get where they supposed to get and do what they supposed to do and be gone when they's supposed to be gone. That's the nature of angels. Just like not hurting nothing is their nature.

But you got to push a man sometime. Unload him out the door cause he been on that Dago Red and his eyes are full of wine and sleep and the house filling up with smoke. She wishes he would wake up enough to whistle a Burn Down the House Blues. She would like that. Oh yes. She could surely listen to that this morning. A Burn Down the House, Burn Down the Town Blues as they sail off that long hill together.

Because somebody has to go down there and tell the truth. Lizabeth's boy didn't kill nobody. He wasn't scared. All he needed was another chance and somebody needs to go down there and tell them. And she was going to do just that: Burn down that last bit of shack on Bruston Hill and tell them what they needed to know. That he ain't killed nobody. That he needed one more chance. That he staked his life on one more chance. They should know all that down there. She'll tell them. She'll make sure they hear. Yes indeed. On her man's arms now. Four good legs now and she's coming. She's coming to tell them he ain't scared no more and they better listen and they better make sure it don't happen so easy ever again.

About the Author

John Edgar Wideman went to school in Pittsburgh and to the universities of Pennsylvania and Iowa. He was a Rhodes scholar at Oxford, was Professor of English at the University of Wyoming, and now teaches at the University of Massachusetts at Amherst. His nonfiction work, *Brothers and Keepers*, was selected as one of the ten best books of 1984 by the editors of *The New York Times Book Review*. The other two books in the Homewood Trilogy, *Damballah* and *Sent for You Yesterday* (winner of the prestigious PEN/Faulkner Award for Fiction), are also available in Vintage.